THE STRENGTH OF MERCY

Shirley Mason

Disclaimer

The Strength of Mercy is fiction. Names, characters, places, and incidents either are the product of the author's imagination or are used fictitiously. Any resemblance to actual persons, living or dead, events, or locales is entirely coincidental.

ISBN 978-0692889114
ISBN   0692889116

Mason Publishing
Green Valley, Arizona

"The quality of mercy is not strained;
It droppeth as the gentle rain from heaven
Upon the place beneath. It is twice blest;
It blesseth him that gives and him that takes:"

The Merchant of Venice
William Shakespeare, 1564 – 1616

The Strength of Mercy

Shirley Mason

1

Edward. He said his name is Edward Fitzpatrick," Lady Charlotte Southway said, her face wore an unusual glow. "You just missed him. He brought in that carton of gentlemen's clothing." She gestured to a large box on a nearby table. "He's a lovely man, Mr. Fitzpatrick, and I hope he returns . . . particularly on a day when I'm here." Lady Southway's face softened into a rare smile. She wouldn't reveal her feelings in such an obvious manner had not Lady Emma Haversham been a good friend. "He first came in over a week ago when he brought in his late father's tuxedo. I guess it's taking him time to let go of his father's belongings."

"Yes. I remember him. I was here that day," Emma said. Emma had come into the shop to help and Lady Southway was filling her in. "Rather handsome I thought. I wonder whether he works around the village. I know what you mean, Charlotte—hoping he comes in when you're here. He is charming. Doesn't put himself forward either. And that blond hair with silver streaks . . . ."

The two women laughed at their silliness. Lady Southway was pleased that she could bring a laugh to Emma; she laughed so seldom since the accident.

Normally shoppers who came in to buy or to donate to Lady Emma Haversham's thrift shop, *New Chance*, were women. It was rare for a man to come in for either purpose.

"A bit odd that, instead of coming in himself, he doesn't send in his wife," said Emma.

"Oh, I was pleased to learn today that he has no wife," Lady Southway twittered just a bit. "He told me that he *had* had one, a clothes designer, who left him for a position with the Fashion Institute in New York. And, he said, as he is a science journalist, and an occasional speaker at functions around England, he needs to be close to our universities to spend a few days each month in Oxford, Cambridge, or London. Thus, he has to live in England. He could take time to visit the States, but not stay. And so, since his wife insisted he find work in the States, he had let her go on without him. Now, five years later, he says that they rarely speak; rarely find time to cross the ocean."

"My, you did learn a good deal about him," Emma said, surprised at Charlotte, normally too reserved to chat up a stranger.

"Yes. No one else was in the shop at the time, and he did seem to want to stay and talk a bit."

"Charlotte, do go on . . . tell me more."

"This past year he's been living alone over in Craig-on-Wold. There, from his neighbor, Oliver, he learned about New Chance and how well it thrives. Of course Oliver attached the shop's success to Lady Claire's windows . . . her designs. Edward said that one evening when he had been invited to join Oliver and Lady Claire for dinner . . . Oliver cooking . . . there had been a discussion about our shop. And, as it was high time that he cleaned out his late father's possessions, and as all New Chance's profits went to charity, he realized that evening exactly where he could place his father's belongings. Though it would be a hard task, his father would have approved."

"Mr. Fitzpatrick told you all that?"

2

"Yes. It was a slow day and finally, I offered him a cup of tea." Lady Southway had begun to remove clothing from Edward's box, which she sorted into separate piles while Emma waited for more about Mr. Fitzpatrick.

"He said he drove over to his father's home in Moreton-on-Marsh and looked around the many rooms of a lifetime spent acquiring lovely furniture, as well as bibelots and paintings and more stuff than one could imagine. An overwhelming task . . . why he had been putting it off."

Emma nodded her head with understanding; she had had much the same task with her Great Aunt Ola's personal effects.

"He had to start somewhere," Lady Southway continued, "and so he decided to gather something, just something, something at hand, and drive the next day to our shop. Nearly the first item that caught his eye was his father's tuxedo, still in the cleaner's bag, hanging on a hook in his father's dressing room."

Emma took a cashmere scarf from one of the piles and folded it. With a lull in shoppers, she could work about arranging things while having a leisurely chat with her good friend and helper, Charlotte.

"His father had been about to attend an awards dinner in his honor when suddenly he died," Lady Southway continued. "Since his father had not often worn the jacket, parting with it would not be painful. That was a start, Edward said, and about all he could manage that day."

With the arrival of customers, Emma and Charlotte turned to ask whether they wanted assistance. It was nearly closing time for New Chance and both Emma and Charlotte were eager to leave for home and for dinner.

2

S ir, you must be content to wait a while longer, a few more days, another week at most, we expect."

Agent Grant Collins, the MI-5 operative most responsible for the earl's wellbeing, sat across the table from him. Of course her Royal Highness's security forces did not expect Lord Simon Haversham to be cloistered without social contact, and Special Agent Grant Collins had been assigned to visit Simon, to help him with any needs he could supply, to bring him newspapers, and spend time in general over tea, sherry, and conversation. And while Simon absorbed the command, Agent Collins poured out sherry into fine crystal glasses that were part of the appointments supplied for Simon while he was held in a secure room at MI-5 Command. Collins looked at the sad, deeply worried expression Lord Haversham wore full-time these days, and his heart, as always, went out to the earl. He wished he could comfort him in some way other than with his company.

"Command knows where the terrorists are and will close in on them soon. It's an absolute requirement, as you can imagine, that they don't make a mistake, that they don't give the men . . . and women, I must add . . . warning. And they must be taken alive."

"But somehow, I must let Emma know I'm safe," Simon said. "She's bound to be in great despair. After all, she received the urn with my supposed remains. What did the agents put into that urn?"

"Ah . . . probably 'sticks and stones and puppy dog tails,' " Agent Collins said, hoping to give his lordship a weak laugh. But it wasn't working. "Sorry, sir . . . bad judgement. I am aware of the despair filling your world right now, but I see relief just around the corner. Please believe this. I honestly do not know what was in the urn, and I hope the assassins don't think to dig it up and find out that it isn't you, or any part of you."

The men sipped sherry while they thought about that possibility, and about the dire need to capture the terrorists before they had that chance. They had already killed two men with a pipe bomb intended for Lord Haversham.

"You must wait another few days, perhaps a week. We know Lady Emma is being watched, and if we let her know you are safe, she'll unintentionally convey her joy. We know that all who come and go from the manor and from New Chance are being watched. Any change in their demeanor will be observed, and they'll be in danger. The saboteurs won't hesitate to kidnap and torture in order to gain their goal." Agent Collins sipped sherry while he waited for the earl's acceptance. "You are the key influence for sanctions on Russia," he continued, "and her agents won't rest until you are out of the way. MI-5, must protect you and your loved ones and as well, your staff. And we know that Russia has her most barbaric operatives here."

"But you say you're on to them, know where they are?" It was a question. His lordship hoped he had heard Agent Collins correctly.

"Yes."

After Lord Simon Appleby Haversham, Fifth Earl of Cav Neumont, had narrowly escaped destruction by a pipe bomb, security had whisked him into safety, and there he stayed, with a guard station just down the hallway. It had been nearly two weeks that he had not been able to let Emma and his adopted son, Peter, or John Britely, his estate manager, or his valet, Pearce, or anyone he knew and loved—but in particular Emma—know he was safe. He felt his deep love and wanted to stretch it across space to enclose her. He had been separated from her twice before: once when his former wife, Lady Claire, had driven Emma off before he had had a chance to keep her for his own, and on another occasion when Emma's former colleague, Brenda, had tried to kill her.

The suite, in which he was securely locked, was elegantly furnished. There were extras for his soul such as a DVD player along with a store of DVDs from the classical period. Excellent meals were brought to him three times a day—if only he could eat. Early on, Agent Collins had become quite upset when he walked in on the earl and saw that he was making a call. Well trained in surprises, Agent Collins had, in one giant step, strode across the room, yanked the phone from Simon and closed it. After that, Simon was not allowed a phone. He understood finally and completely the dire situation he and Emma were in. The terrorists, likely questioning whether Simon had been destroyed, had men in the area and were watching. If they thought Emma had any knowledge at all about Simon, other than that he was deceased, they would close in on her. Her life, or Peter's, or John's, or any of the staff, could be at risk. So, Lord Haversham had to stray put and quietly grieve to himself, while knowing about the deep hurt with which Emma and Peter had to live. Since he saw almost no one throughout the days, he was grateful for Agent Collins' visits. And Collins—also visiting Emma, and occasionally New Chance—would bring Simon news.

"The other day, I was amazed to see a man working at New Chance," Agent Collins said. "So last night when I popped round to the manor, Lady Charlotte Southway happened to be there. I asked about him, and she said that on several occasions he had brought in donations that belonged to his deceased father. And that the last time he came in with an armful, she had been working alone, swamped with customers . . . with the return of milder weather, customers had ventured out to shop . . . and she had been unable to easily handle the volume. People were standing around waiting to be helped; waiting for someone to take their money. She said that she had put in a call to Lady Haversham, but she hadn't arrived before the man, whose name is Edward Fitzpatrick, saw the tight situation and asked Lady Southway to let him help. She said that she was so relieved she allowed him to take customers' money."

Regretting the worried expression overtaking the earl, Agent Collins wished he had not mentioned Mr. Fitzpatrick. He wished he could give Lord Haversham news to lighten his heart, not to cause him more unease. But it was too late now and he went on with the rest of the story. "Lady Southway said that when Lady Haversham arrived and saw the good help Mr. Fitzpatrick gave, and after speaking to him for a bit, agreed that if he liked, he could help at New Chance again, that it would be nice to have a man's effort. Moreover, Mr. Fitzpatrick is a friend of Lady Claire's and her beau, Mr. Oliver somebody, and they had recommended New Chance to Mr. Fitzpatrick as a good place to take his father's possessions." Agent Collins couldn't decide whether the earl looked slightly relieved, and so he rushed on. "Apparently Lady Claire is devoted to New Chance, has found new life in decorating New Chance's display window, and she would not send an unsavory character to the shop. So, though as you know, New Chance has never advertised for help, has asked only known friends to volunteer there, Mr. Fitzpatrick was not to be considered a stranger off the street."

Although this further explanation from Agent Collins did not erase the frown and sadness from Lord Haversham's brow, he did seem to relax just a bit; he trusted Emma's decisions.

3

The wind seemed heavy with secret messages as it swirled around Lady Emma Haversham. She took slow, hesitant, even grave steps, as she listened, trying to hear what the wind had in mind. She was headed to the chapel. Her last visit there had been for Simon's memorial. Although she had accepted the fact that he was gone, destroyed in an act of terrorism, her acceptance had nicks about it, cracks, something incomplete. Openings in her belief would occur to whisper that Simon was still about somewhere: the phone call with the brief—so brief she couldn't be sure she had heard—*The Holberg Suite*. *The Holberg Suite*! A favorite. They had listened to it on many occasions. And when, after MI-5 had told her Simon had been killed, and the phone by her bed had rung, had she really heard three faint seconds of *The Holberg* before the line went dead? Life and love had continued at Cav Neumont Manor without Simon, but just under the life and love, she still heard the sound of that tantalizing phone call.

Sir Simon was said to have been killed by a terrorist attack as he was leaving Westminster. Destruction, the authorities had reported, was so thorough, that few identifying remains could be found, and, contained in a sealed urn, they had brought those to Emma. As well, as they were driving out, the lives of two other members of

Parliament had been taken that day. A memorial to honor Simon's life had been erected on the grounds of Cav Neumont Manor with conviction that he would never be there again.

As Emma walked, Major led ahead, and Schrödinger kept pace with her as though they, cherished dog and cat, knew her destination. Emma loved this walk that took her through the gardens' round-about and passed laurels before reaching the chapel entry. Inside the chapel she could feel Simon's presence, but then there was not a moment when she did not feel his presence. What was different about the chapel? Perhaps it was just its absolute quiet. Whatever it was, it caused her feeling for Simon's presence to become stronger.

In the chapel, she took a seat and looked around at its Baroque beauty. Simon had had it rebuilt according to the design of the original chapel from three-hundred years back, when the occupying earl had it destroyed. Lady Joan, it was said, had begun her existence as the manor's ghost at that time, wailing in anguish for the loss of the chapel. After Simon, always one to reach out, to comfort, had the chapel restored, the wailing stopped. Still Lady Joan's presence about the manor was a frequent, even positive occurrence; she hadn't wanted to leave, and seemed to be loved as much as the other residents of the manor. And now, if Emma could believe it, Lady Joan stood at the pulpit calmly watching her. Did Lady Joan actually have a smile?

Emma gave her thoughts of Simon over to thoughts about her duties for the day, and rose to leave. Major and Schrödinger knew this signal and preceded Emma out the door. They also missed Simon, and seeming to share the loss, they would accompany Emma wherever they could. Back inside the manor, Emma moved into the breakfast room. The long day of work at New Chance needed a good start with Mrs. Ogilvy, the kitchen manager's, excellent breakfast. And it was always a pleasure for Emma to start her morning with Peter, home from university, John Britely, estate manager, and his wife, Hannah, and the much appreciated staff serving at table: Emma's world. Her loved ones. In addition to her son, Joshua, attending university in the States, these were the people with whom she continued life.

"Hannah, I'm ready to leave for the shop," Emma said. "I'll walk down . . . I think I see sunshine breaking through. Would you like to walk with me?"

Cav Neumont Manor had been the site for joinings, as well as for breakings. Hannah had temporarily moved from Wickenbird Farm to the Manor to help Emma at the shop, and with her sewing and mending skills, she had stayed on for a bit. Although, it had been a slowly growing realization, John and she had welcomed the opportunity to be around each other, take walks together.

"I'm ready, Emma, and yes, I'll join you for the walk. I look forward to our customers. Volunteering at New Chance has opened up my life."

On their way out, Emma picked up a bundle of donations waiting on a front table. Often there was one gathered by one of the manor's staff. New Chance, run completely by volunteers, offered gently used goods, mostly clothing, priced shockingly low, but as well, books and a small assortment of treasures, all of which were donations. A popular shop, New Chance attracted customers from villages round-about; they came to buy something they thought they had always wanted, and would bring a donation, something they no longer needed, and would tarry a bit for a cup of tea. New Chance had become a favorite landmark for the village of Cav Neumont, and actually earned a profit that was turned back into the parish

On the walk to the village Emma thought about how events had come to pass: So many connections. Cav Neumont Manor seemed to have love and connections evolving in all directions, except for her own: Simon wasn't there. Her heart warmed with the happy situations all around her. Hannah and John had come together at the manor. And Sophia and Mars. And even though she hoped not to have Lady Mardling, with her growing closeness to Count Bianco, leave the village and thus no longer volunteer at the shop—Emma was happy to see that Lady Mardling's face, formerly stiff and disdainful, now was relaxed with an aspect of happiness.

And what about Lady Claire, the former Lady Haversham? She was an amazing turnabout, Emma thought. It was but little more than a year ago when, with her various schemes, Lady Claire had tried to separate her from Simon. Claire had tried to spoil much that went on at the manor. Yet, now she was all kindness—seemed to have a new companion, Oliver—and was a marvel, a miracle with the shop's window display. Once a rather frivolous soul darting about over the globe running up debt, Lady Claire seemed to have found peace through working at New Chance.

She had come down from London bent on inspecting the shop to see what she would change—if it were up to her—when her old friend, Lady Mardling, one of the volunteers that day, suggested to Claire that instead of standing around, she might get busy and help with the display window. The volunteers had no time to do it up in an interesting manner, and it was rather an eyesore. Thus, Claire found amusement in putting her heart into New Chance's display window and in the process had created a winsome show that caused villagers to gather about and even to take photos.

Each had someone to think about, to care for—but not Emma. Though she loved John Britely and Peter, and now even Hannah, as family, there was that gaping hole for Simon.

It was a slow day at New Chance—an unusually hot spring day, that kept everyone cooling within the stones of their cottages. Emma and Hannah hadn't much to do. The piles of donations that, after the village fair ended, had come in from vendors, and needed sorting and sometimes polishing or ironing or mending, but especially organizing and pricing, had been attended to; the overflow carefully folded and stored on shelves in the back storage room, ready to be brought out when space opened up.

"Hannah, if you don't mind," Emma said with her questioning face, "I'd like to walk through the village for a bit."

"Do . . . it's such a slow day, I'll be fine here alone."

Most of the year New Chance was full of shoppers from the time it opened until the time it closed. It was just the recent, quite hot days that provided a break in the work. With its regular volunteers—Lady Emma Haversham, who had started the shop, Lady Mardling, and Lady Southway—New Chance throve.

As Emma walked down Main Street, she noticed again the man: the one she had seen a few times before. A stranger, she thought—not a villager, and though he kept his distance, he appeared to follow her with his eyes. Then after a bit he would turn away, or take a seat on a bench, speak into his mobile, open up his newspaper, and appear to forget her. She mostly saw him when she arrived at the shop to open up, or at five as she was leaving. Someday, Emma vowed, she would ask him what he was about, where did he come from, or where did he live. Major, the Labrador who would wait under the tea table at the shop, walked along beside Emma. A gentle dog, he was never a threat to shoppers. In fact if someone saw him, his or her instinct would be to pet Major. And this day the stranger wanted to pet Major. He saw Emma, folded his paper, stood and turned in her direction. He walked up to Major and reached to pet the dog. He seemed to be quite confident that Major would be friendly. Emma—though she heard herself, heard the words when she would ask the man about himself—was speechless. Now all she could find to say was, "His name is Major, and I am Lady Haversham."

"Ah . . . he looks like a Major." The man looked up at Emma and smiled. "Tyler Brotherton, and it's my pleasure to meet you."

He petted Major again, and soon, feeling uncomfortable and uncertain about his position, and finding a pause in the colloquy, said good-day, tipped his hat, turned and walked toward the inn.

Was he staying in the village, Emma wondered. It was only recently that she had been seeing him about. Had he not walked off so quickly she would have asked him how he liked their village, and had he toured the manor? With the return of summer, and the return of tourists, Cav Neumont Manor would again be opening for the public—only certain areas, and only at certain times, a bit more limited than in former times, before the tragedy. And for this opening, Emma had an appointment with Troy, the manor's former groundsman.

4

Troy and Corky were back from Scotland. Troy, a rascal sometimes, but not at all a malicious man, had lost his better judgement back before Emma met Lord Haversham, and had played a hoax on her. Though at the time he was Lord Haversham's groundsman, Troy had impersonated the earl. His tomfoolery had almost kept Emma and Simon from ever meeting, but fate had looked kindly on them, and Troy's scheme was discovered in good time. After that, Lord Haversham dispatched Troy to a farm the earl owned in Scotland.

Sorry indeed, but grateful to still have employment, Troy had moved with his sweetheart, Corky, to the farm, had run it well, turned a profit, and trained a good manager. Now, they wanted to move back to the village of Cav Neumont, a desire prompted by Corky, who complained about the cold weather at the farm. But the occasion that forced Troy back to Cav Neumont was the news about the earl's death. Troy, contrite and sorry for the deception he had played on Emma, wanted to help. He was back to help.

"I've known you as Emma, and now I know that I must know you as Lady Emma," he said, when he asked her for an interview. He had helped with Sir Simon's memorial, stepping in where needed. Emma saw his grief, understood that he would not again engage in foul play. He had in fact apologized to her and to his lordship, back before their marriage.

"I know you have a new groundsman," he said, "and I respect that of course. I come to ask . . . to hope . . . there might be another position I can fill here at the manor. I've always loved the estate."

Emma, her heart already softened toward Troy, thought for a minute. Then, "Troy, our docent will be moving into a retirement home. I know from the past, that you aren't familiar with the manor's artifacts . . . those the public sees, and if you can study our sculpture and paintings, learn just the basics about them, and if Mr. Britely agrees, and I feel certain he will out of consideration for the good service you have given the estate, you may have that position. The public asks questions, you know. And you'll need to look smart, and will want to sound informed and knowledgeable. I think it's the only position coming open."

Troy's head energetically bobbed itself up and down. "Certainly, milady." This was a change he had to make for her—going from speaking to her as Emma to speaking to her title. He had already learned many lessons, and continued to learn many more, in particular that of Lady Emma's forgiving him, her kind heart.

"Troy, where are you and Corky living?"

"Corky was able to rent her former room in the village. We're living there."

"I'll check with Mr. Britely, but I think we have a vacant flat off the north courtyard. Perhaps he can find other ways for you to help at the manor in addition to acting as docent, and you and Corky will be welcome to take a flat here. But, as I said, Mr. Britely is in charge of that. I'll ask him to please speak to you."

Troy felt moisture behind his eyes, and made his best effort to hold it back. Still, he had to pull out his handkerchief and dab his eyes. Words failed him, were inadequate; his relief and delight inexpressible.

"You'll have much studying to do. Mr. Britely will give you the catalog to study, and will let you know about the flat."

With the slightest bow, and without another word, for he couldn't find one with a steady voice, Troy spun and left before Lady Emma saw his emotion.

As Emma watched him leave, she mused about how things had worked out: she knew the flat was available, and she would speak to John right away. She knew Troy would give good service. Yes, he had been a scoundrel initially, but she could see into his earnestness that he had learned from his errors.

When she spoke to John Britely about hiring Troy for docent, she promised (sticking out her neck) that Troy would study to be versed in the rooms and treasures the public would tour. Although John did trust Emma's instincts, he knew about Troy's previous chicanery, and had doubts on some level about the man's trustworthiness. Still, he didn't want to deny any request of Emma's.

"Let me think about it, Emma. I keenly remember the man's history. Still, he has given Sir Simon good service, both here as the previous groundsman, and more recently running the farm in Scotland." He pinched his nose while he continued to think.

Emma waited, trying not to influence.

"I know he's at heart a good man," John said. "I know he grieves along with the rest of us for Simon." John took a long pause.

Emma continued to wait. She had enormous respect for whatever John thought, for whatever he decided.

"Let's go ahead and give him a chance," he said. "I can't imagine his being docent, though. But we need one. Let's see what he can do. I'll accumulate the literature for him to study."

Emma wore one of her rare smiles these days, for she did want to help Troy.

"But Emma, let's not move him to a flat on the estate just yet. Should he not work out, it might be difficult to ask him to leave. I understand he comes with his companion, Corky. I've seen her at The Bucket. Apparently they are renting a room in the village . . . let's leave them there for now."

5

Edward, even though he had to drive over from Craig-on-Wold, enjoyed his day volunteering at New Chance. Customers took to him quite easily. He was an attraction: tall and sturdy, with blonde hair, and a lovely sharp profile supporting a ready smile. He could even be an innocent tease when he thought it appropriate. He took the days to volunteer when Lady Charlotte Southway worked. She was easy to work with, didn't run at the mouth during the slow hours. Would busy herself about sorting, arranging or folding; always concerned about the shop's appearance. Edward found that he enjoyed being there with her, and sometimes he found ways to make her laugh. And volunteering at the shop, contact with those close to the Havershams, fed straight into his covert assignment. And on some days Lady Haversham would be there.

"Did Emma hire you particularly to annoy me?" Lady Southway asked one day after he had issued an ironic remark to her about being "Lady-tuck-and-fold-em." But she had backed up her question with the most friendly grin. She loved Edward's chuckle and it was welcoming to have a quiet hour for comradery with him; a slow hour, Lady Southway was fussier then usual about tidying cabinets and shelves.

"Have you noticed that man?" Edward was gesturing out the display window to a man sitting on a bench across the road. "I have seen him before . . . just waiting around it appears. If I could believe it, he watches our shop as though he expects something to happen here."

Lady Southway moved to the front to look, and glanced across the road to the man in question. "Yes, I've seen him a few times. Perhaps he's a tourist . . . I think he knows that we are staring at him." She turned away from the window. "Perhaps he's obsessed with the skimpily-dressed model Lady Claire has arranged in the window. A bikini in Cav Neumont!" She thought for a moment while Edward continued to watch the man. "Well, summer has been looking in," she said, "and it's a bit warmer. The manor has a pool, and Lady Claire used to live there years ago. Perhaps she was thinking of that. Beach balls, beach towels. Sand. We do not have any of those to sell."

"Sand! How do we sell sand?" Edward laughed. "Do we have buckets? My dear Charlotte, would you show me the sand so I can offer some to the next customer who comes in for a beach towel."

"The sand, my dear, is all in your eyes." She wasn't prepared for his next remark.

"Sand in my eyes! I think I should take you to dinner so that I can tell you how I acquired eye-sand, and you can tell me more about what goes on in Cav Neumont that I haven't yet learned. Say this evening . . . I don't want to waste more time in ignorance."

Lady Southway's surprise prevented a ready reply. In the past, she would have had a barbed reply—that is, before she had a chance to realize she had an invitation from a lovely man. Now, she was able only to stare at him.

"Say after we close we ankle over to either The Meridian, or to The Bucket. Your preference, milady."

Lady Southway pulled together her nerves, organized her surprise into composure and said, "Oh let's."

"Right. So don't speak to me again about sand, buckets and what all, until I have a pint before me to help handle this folderol."

"The stranger is moving on," Charlotte said as she turned back to the window. "Perhaps in response to our spotting him."

Edward watched Lady Southway as she watched the man on the green. He recognized that the sand said to be in his eyes, might relate to his growing fondness for her; Charlotte, he called her when serious; Lady Southway when he was teasing. She had a rather severe face, but when he teased her it softened up revealing a delightful hidden self of which he wanted to see more. He looked forward to dinner with her when they could have private, getting-to-know-you talk. Still, he would be on guard to prevent her knowing him too well.

6

Tyler Brotherton, reading the paper, and sometimes speaking on his mobile, still took time to watch New Chance. In fact, when he seemed to be reading, as he sat on the village green bench, he had one eye on the shop. Even when ordering a sandwich from the bakery, he would wait near the window keeping that eye out to see who came and went. His Russian handler had ordered him to watch Lady Haversham—he had been given information about her, knew that she had started the shop, and worked there three or four days every week. The Russians, not convinced that Lord Haversham had been killed in the explosion, wanted the earl out of the way so seriously that in order to gain information, they placed several men in the field to watch the Havershams; in particular Lady Emma Haversham and the shop, New Chance.

When Brotherton had introduced himself to Emma, it was plain to see her pain. If the earl were still alive, surely she was completely unaware. Nevertheless, Lord Haversham—were he in hiding, might try to contact her. As an MI-5 mole, secretly acting for the Russians, Brotherton had not been told exactly what MI-5 knew. Just follow orders, watch Lady Haversham and the shop, and if anything changes, report it. Ironically, both MI-5 *and* the Russians ordered him to watch Lady Haversham. After the shop closed for the day, Tyler would move to The Meridian Inn, where he stayed temporarily, or to The Bucket Arms for dinner.

On this night at The Bucket, Barney, the bartender, was speaking to a woman seated at the bar. Loud with complaints, the astonishing woman wagged her disgruntled head about while telling Barney the story of her life—at least, it sounded so; Tyler was near enough to hear.

"The deli wouldn't give me back my old job," Corky carped. "And with Troy's meager starting pittance at the manor, I've got to find meself work somewhere."

"Well, Corky, that's what happens when you do a stint out of town. Leads them not to trust you so, thinking you might leave again."

Corky let her cigarette smoke curl up around her face as she thought about that. "Show them, I will. Troy's looking into work for me at the manor. That'll be easier; they're a soft bunch. Then, he says, we might even be able to move into one of the manor's flats . . . you know, the staff quarters in one of the courtyards. Have you been there? Taken the tour?"

"Nay. Always at work, I am. Live in the other direction." This was a good time for Barney to ask why he hadn't seen Troy lately. "How's Troy keeping? He's been in only once since you returned from Scotland."

"Ah. His face is buried in books and catalogues. He's not free for talk or for anything else." She rolled her eyes. S'why I come in without him."

"What's keeping his face buried?"

"He has to study; learn about the manor's splendid stuff. Statues and stuff. You know he's going to be the docent, once he learns the talk . . . how to answer questions."

"I wouldn't think that'd be up his line."

"Frankly, can't meself see him doing that. Was the only job at the manor they could find for him at this time.

23

And he wants to work at the manor; he loves that place. He says it's a miracle they let him try for the position. You know that he was groundsman there for twenty years. Don't know what made the earl send him off to Scotland."

Barney thought he knew: Troy had once bragged to Barney about his scheme to impersonate the earl. And by doing so, Troy had nearly prevented Emma and the earl from meeting. But on that, Barney would remain silent.

Although the woman and the Barney's conversation stopped there, they had given Tyler Brotherton a new idea. Corky—he heard Barney call her that—looked to be free and easy. Perhaps she would be open to another friendship, namely his own. He planned to follow her out when she left the tavern, and attempt a conversation with her toward the possibility that she would indeed become employed at the manor. Women found him attractive; perhaps his charms would appeal to Corky enough to enable him to befriend her, get her to talk. An inside ear at the manor would be splendid. The comrades would praise him for establishing such a contact. And as it had been a recent decision to assist the enemy—the money had been too great a temptation—this was his first assignment. A non-violent assignment, he would only be reporting what went on at the manor, or at the shop, seeking clues to the earl's possible survival.

He had to wait. Whatever Corky had to go home to, Troy studying, or—Tyler could only guess—she was not in a hurry to leave. And Tyler, a slim, distinguished looking man who watched his weight, was required to order another ale, and another, and even dessert, a rich compote of some sort. Finally, when Corky did pay her tab to leave, Tyler had had so much ale and profusion of sweets that he fairly staggered out behind her. Outside, slightly on purpose, he *slightly* fell onto her.

She didn't mind at all as she took a look at his lovely face. "I think you've been into it a bit, love. Would you like to take my arm?"

He knew exactly what he was doing as he let his weight fall softly onto her. "Right. I could use a hand over to The Meridian where I had a room the last I checked."

"Happy to oblige, I am." Though Corky was inclined to be true to Troy, she wasn't married to him. They merely had an agreement that they were partnered, more or less, for now. She guessed she still had her looks, and felt a pleasant flush that this man seemed to like her. "See you in now," she reluctantly said at the inn.

"Thank you, my dear. May I repay the favor tomorrow? Say with an early dinner at The Bucket? What say meet me there at five?"

"My pleasure, love. Until then." And she saw Tyler into the door, turned and walked over to the house where she and Troy rented a room. When Troy let her in, she said nothing about the encounter with the handsome stranger; her little secret and a surprising one at that. She was doing nothing wrong by looking forward to dinner with the stranger. She hoped he remembered.

The next evening she arrived at The Bucket Arms early so she could arrange herself just so on the bar stool, her knee showing just a bit, her hair freshly smoothed against the wind's effort to disarrange it. And she had changed into all black with revealing décolleté; black made a good contrast to her red hair and smooth white skin. When Tyler stepped into the tavern Corky resisted looking to see who had come in. She posed just so with, she hoped, a touch of nonchalant elegance.

Tyler wasn't remiss; he made certain she knew that he admired the effort. But for all her effort, the dinner passed in a non-spectacular manner: Tyler Brotherton, though surely flirting, had talked to her in only general terms until she wondered whether indeed he had any interest in her. If not, why had he asked for her company? Earlier, she hadn't considered what she thought would happen, what moves Tyler would make—still she had expected something rather than nothing and she had enjoyed looking forward to a flirtatious meal with Mr. Brotherton. It was not frequent—actually, it was infrequent—that a gentleman paid her attention, especially a gentleman of Mr. Brotherton's rank. He had said he was single, and was a Security Engineer on holiday. Not fresh either; hadn't made a pass at her, but definitely found her interesting. No one else found her interesting except Troy, and she was so used to that, she could fit that on the tip of her spoon and flick it across the room, she could. And when she arrived home Troy was still studying, his eyes fixed on a page before him; he hardly acknowledged her arrival.

"Goodnight, dear," he said. "I'll turn in shortly." He hadn't much to say to Corky, and he did not ask where she had been. He knew she had been at The Bucket, their old hangout. He did not expect her to stay home when all he wanted to do was study; he took the learning seriously. Learning had before been a mysterious, unavailable effort, now he felt himself rising in the world, entering into another class. And, though it had been slow coming about, he was growing impressed with the importance of the manor's accoutrements. Words like callipygian, neoclassical, Hellenistic. His head was swimming with words and letters all in a jumble. Surely, though, some of it was sinking in.

"Do," she said. "I'll have a time of it trying to sleep with the light on."

The next few days went on in a similar manner until one evening when Corky came in from The Bucket, Troy said,

"Hello, dear. Pour yourself a cup of coffee, and sit down. I have news that I hope you'll find to be good news."

Corky looked at him with a question.

"Mr. Britely says Mrs. Ogilvy can use your help in the kitchen. I assured him you knew a lot about cooking."

That's a stretch, Corky thought. Working at the video shop had taught her how to work a vending machine.

"It will be five days a week on a rotating schedule."

"Rotating schedule?"

"That's the deal. People at the manor are served six days a week. I think it'll work out that you'll have every other weekend off, and your work day will end at four." Troy didn't think it was a good idea just yet to point out that every weekend throughout the summer he would be working as docent for the manor's public tours.

Corky knew she'd better not object. She needed Troy in her life, and they might soon be moving into one of the flats in the north courtyard, over the stables. Soon. She would give the kitchen a try.

"You start tomorrow. Mrs. Ogilvy is expecting you at eight in the morning, and the butler, Brooks, or his assistant, Hadley, will show you the way to the kitchen. Mrs. Ogilvy is pleasant; I know her from times in the past when I ate with the staff. It's a walloping good opportunity. I might ask for the chance to swop with you," he teased. "I'll drive you over."

As Troy would be studying a short while longer, Corky said goodnight and turned into bed with dreams of the news she would have for Mr. Brotherton. When he had asked whether she could meet him again at The Bucket for supper of course she had said yes, and quickly. Then she realized she should have been more subtle, but the word, with a highly fluid mind of its own, had rushed out.

The next evening, she was again rewarded with Tyler Brotherton's interest, for his eyes lit up when she entered and he seemed to be waiting for her. He picked up his drink and led her to a rear booth. In her excitement, almost before he could take her wrap, she began to relate her new position: working in the manor's kitchen.

"So far I'm just learning my way around," she said.

"Tell me. I want to know all about it."

"Lor, why would you be interested in that?" He was supposed to be interested in her, not in the kitchen.

"I like knowing how a huge mansion such as that functions. The organizing of it must be a marvel. Did you see Lady Haversham?" He felt uncomfortable, slimy, even. He had the sudden sensation that he was not cut out for spying. He had trained for the opposite end—security. Security *from* spies. How did he get started in this anyway? He had to think back. Ask himself just what was he doing. Meanwhile, until he sorted it out, he would carry on.

"No. I wonder if she *ever* goes down to the kitchen. It runs without her." Corky became curious. "How do you know about Lady Haversham? Even I didn't know about her, not really . . . that is until she opened New Chance."

"Someone at The Meridian said I should take the tour through the manor. Her name came up." He wanted any news about the Havershams but he couldn't let on.

Two days later, to Troy and Corky's delight, a flat had been made ready for them. There were two rooms running from east to west, furnished thoughtfully with basic but good appointments, a tiny kitchen complete with colorful dishtowels, a bath with hot water, and there were lovely views in both directions.

"Imagine," Corky said, "we have our own bath and hot water!" She had never had it so good. It took but fifteen minutes to move in and arrange her small supply of clothing and cosmetics, and then she studied the views. A view! They had a view! She felt as though she were living in the manor house itself.

So, it was that Troy and Corky were able to occupy a flat on the estate, upstairs over the stables in the north courtyard; quite handy for Troy as docent. Corky, losing her job in the village by moving with Troy to Scotland, was genuinely pleased to have employment at the manor, about which she had never heard anything but good. And she needed the income.

"I'm learning to sauté," she said to Tyler after her second day in the kitchen. She had hoped to meet Tyler at The Bucket. He had ordered dinner for her. "I can't believe how easy about the work the cooks are. No one yells!"

"They have my full admiration," Tyler said.

"To start, my hours in the kitchen are from eight to four, and with me mate always studying, after work I have to get out, and so I take a golf cart here." She wanted to explain to Tyler that, though they had moved into a flat four miles up the lane, she could still get to The Bucket evenings; Troy had the use of one of the manor's golf carts. She hoped Tyler picked up on her hint. She couldn't suggest that he have dinner with her again, but that was her intention. "I can eat with the staff but Troy wants to keep studying so I bring him a plate," she explained lest Tyler wondered about these details. "He wants everything memorized so when a tourist asks him about a painting or statue, he can quick spout out the facts. It's the hardest job he's had, and at first he didn't know whether he was up for it, but his big head is growing. He's stacking facts into that lazy brain of his until me thinks he'll explode. In only a week from now he starts working as docent."

Finally, Corky told Troy that while he studied, she sometimes talked to a man at The Bucket.

"Excellent, my dear," he said without really taking in her disclosure. "I know I'm not much company these days. But someday I'll know it all and won't have to study another minute. We've stepped into good luck, my dear," Troy said. "We must appreciate these opportunities."

He had become a know-it-all and rather proud, Corky thought—loudly spouting strange words. It was more amusing to be with Mr. Brotherton, Tyler, she called him. All Tyler did was ask simple questions, such as—did she ever see Peter, Lord Haversham's adopted son? Or Mr. Britely? Showed he was interested in her world. When she asked why he had so much interest in the Havershams and staff, Tyler said that he was researching village life in the Cotswolds. He could write, and did on occasion, and had thought about applying himself to writing essays.

That made sense, Corky thought, a good reason why he was curious. She felt proud to be able to provide any topic she had to hand.

7

Agent Collins had brought a chess set, and Simon and he engaged in fierce competition. Neither was up to practice and so neither had an unfair advantage.

"I don't know how long I can endure without Emma," Simon said on one of these visits. "Nor she without me, and I grieve for her and for her health, sad as she is bound to be."

"You know I call on her as part of my orders," said Agent Collins. "She tries not to wear her sadness, but it shows like bumps on a shiver. Yet she rises to her responsibilities. She sees that the shop goes on, and she works with Mr. Britely to see that the manor thrives." He wanted to give the earl some hope; still he dreaded giving him false hope. How much should he reveal? He debated with his own wisdom for a bit. "Two of the suspects' hideouts are known and of course watched, and they'll soon be captured." He prayed he wasn't premature with such risky news. And while Simon absorbed this information, Agent Collins hoped the earl wouldn't notice that he had made a wise chess move. "They want to take them alive. Then you'll be released from your misery." He wished he could do something to put a real smile on the earl's face, but he had already said enough, perhaps too much.

With this news Simon wanted to jump up and shout, but a quiet warning intervened—much could go wrong—he would save his exhilaration for final results. He simply gave Collins a nod of affirmation and turned his attention to the chess move the agent had just made. He saw that his own queen was now in jeopardy; perhaps he could distract Collins. "I grieve as well for my pets: Schrödinger and Major. Not so much for Major, for that wonderful lab fits in with everyone at the manor and won't miss me as much as will Schrödinger. That cat tends to follow me around. He has a tower near me in the dining room, and he's politely waiting there when I come in to eat. He expects a few morsels from my plate. I wonder how he's doing without me. Will someone else give him such attention? Or will Schrödinger let someone else? Even in the midst of all this horror, I worry about my pets."

"I often see Schrödinger and Major," Agent Collins said, "when I visit the manor."

Simon made a chess move that saved his queen.

Agent Collins put pet thoughts aside until he made another clever chess move. "Nice pets. They seem to be quite civilized; sit around at our feet while Lady Haversham, Mr. Britely, and I converse. They know that we are about to catch the terrorists, and are always happy to see me with any news. Next time, I'll give Schrödinger a special petting . . . he'll sense that's it's from you. He probably detects your pheromones on my clothing, just from my sitting here with you. Ah, I wondered why he was so intent on rubbing my pants cuff . . . that's why . . . Schrödinger knows you are alive, for when I left here last, I went straight there."

Simon made a chess move, while he thought about that: Schrödinger must wonder why he doesn't come home.

The next day Agent Grant arrived at Cav Neumont Manor exactly at six and was shown up to the library where

Emma, John Britely, and Hannah were waiting dinner. Always pleased to see him, they knew the agent cared about them, worried about their welfare, and he provided relief from their own conversations that had grown stale with thoughts always on Simon.

"So Schrödinger was his lordship's particular friend?" Agent Collins asked.

"Indeed," John Britely said. "Followed Simon around just as you would expect a dog to do. That cat misses Simon as much as we do."

Agent Collins picked up the cat and held him on his lap. Surprisingly, though he was not used to being picked up, Schrödinger did not protest. When Emma asked Agent Collins to stay for dinner, he said his family waited for him, thank you though—he must be on his way. Schrödinger accidently, or perhaps on purpose, followed him out to his car.

Brooks, seeing Agent Collins to the door, paid scant attention to the cat following the man down the steps, for the pet had the run of both inside and outside. However, Brooks noticed, that when Agent Collins drove away around the circle, Schrödinger was nowhere in sight. Agent Collins had scooped up the cat with one quick swing, whisked him into the car, and had driven off before a second thought could be fashioned by man or beast.

"Sorry I'm a bit late, dear." Collins said over his mobile to his wife. "You'll be surprised to see what I stopped off for." And when he arrived home and went in the door, he carried cat, cat food, and a cat pan with cat litter. "This is not for us, dear," he said to his shocked wife. "It's for a very sad man for whom I am responsible. This is his much-loved pet." He could explain nothing more, but his wife knew not to ask, and not to expect more.

When Agent Collins arrived the next day at Simon's suite, as soon as he knocked and unlocked the door, and saw Simon with his usual sad face sitting across the room, he reached in Schrödinger, who, taking exactly one second to know Simon was in the room, sped over to him and leaped onto his lap. His purr could have been heard from the hallway. Simon had a tear as he reached down and picked up the animal. Home, it was something from home: something very dear.

"I'll be back in five minutes with Schrödinger's equipment," Agent Collins said. And soon he returned with the litter box, and cat food. "I didn't have a chance to find out what he prefers to eat . . . I'm open to suggestions; I'll buy whatever it is. I want to see the look on their faces when I submit a bill to Accounting for cat food and a litter box with litter. Do you think I must explain that it's not for you?" Sometimes, as now, Collins could manage to pull a slight smile from Sir Simon.

"I doubt your accounting will even notice," Simon said, "so used to your group, they are. Or, you might say I've taken a turn for cat food. No, you cannot say that . . . not knowing how long I'll still need the chef's services, we cannot offend him." Though he keenly felt despair, he could still rise to return a quip.

"I'll say you're used to midnight snacks of cat food. That'll fix them."

"Or, maybe it'll fix me." Simon said.

"No, they won't think a thing, so used to the eccentricities of the landed gentry."

While Simon and Schrödinger looked more than content saying hello to each other, Agent Collins set about filling the litter box, filling a bowl with water, opening a can of cat food and scooping out a bit. He had missed nothing.

For a moment Simon thought only of holding his treasured pet. But as he did, he pictured those at the manor who would miss Schrödinger; *really* miss him, and who would worry about him. "I'm not so certain this is a good idea," he said to the agent.

Grant looked up to see a new kind of worry on Simon's face.

"Why so, sir?"

"I know how Emma will look for him; she'll have the place turned upside-down. She'll have no peace . . . nor will anyone else at the manor."

The air hung still and heavy while the two men thought about this, Simon still holding Schrödinger close.

"Sir, I have an idea," Agent Collins said. "In a day or two, after you've had good company with Schrödinger, I'll take him back. Lady Haversham and the others at the manor will just think he was off hunting."

That might work, Simon thought. Still, Schrödinger was not known for leaving and hunting. He preferred to be in by a fire, and if possible sitting by Emma's, or his own feet. But, of course, with himself gone, Schrödinger might have a different routine.

"I must pop in regularly, sir," the agent said, "to visit Lady Haversham, both to make sure she's okay, as well as to learn whether they've seen anything strange about the manor. I can drop him off as I arrive." The agent watched Simon as he waited for his decision.

"Right. Perhaps your idea will work. Actually, I don't see why not. If you can be bothered. And Schrödinger might also be at peace with that arrangement, knowing I'm safe here. He's smart enough for that. Probably the best plan . . . if I'm to have his company."

So it was decided that Schrödinger would spend a day or two with Simon, then be carried back to the manor, and quite soon after, Agent Collins would—if he could find the cat, which should be easy enough, his always sitting with Emma around the fire—fetch him again. He would have to hope that Schrödinger would follow him out to the car so no one would witness his capture. And since, in the past Schrödinger had followed him, Agent Collins thought his plan would work. In time, and he hoped it wouldn't actually be too long a time until Lord Haversham could safely return to the manor, Lady Haversham would stop worrying about the cat, and accept that Schrödinger might wander off for a few days. Stranger things had happened—especially with cats.

If only Agent Collins could have known that when he drove the cat in to Simon, he was being watched by someone who would put that information to good use.

"The manor cat has gone missing," Corky said, her brows lifted in jest with this item that she thought Mr. Brotherton, Tyler, could use in one of his essays.

"Missing! The cat missing?"

"You said that twice . . . the cat blocked your tongue, or something?" Corky had several times now met Brotherton, and felt teasingly comfortable with him. "You can put that in one of your essays: 'Cat, beloved pet of slain earl, goes off to find him.' Can't you weave that into one of your village stories?"

"Good point. So happy you mentioned it. Since when has the cat gone missing?"

"Don't ask me. When they came down to the kitchen to eat, I heard Hadley ask the butler, Brooks, where the cat was, Schrofer, or some crazy name. All that fuss over a cat! But Brooks didn't seem to care much. And strange thing is I'm certain that earlier in the day I saw that cat in the kitchen."

Tyler Brotherton ordered another drink for Corky while he thought about this. Was this significant? Why? Could this be important enough to report to Blinov? Surely not, but he had been ordered to report anything that might be considered unusual.

"How are Lady Haversham and the son holding up? Have you heard?" he asked, hoping to hear something else significant. If they were hiding Lord Haversham, it ought to show on their faces, in their demeanor. One wouldn't expect them to appear broken-hearted if they knew the earl was alive.

"About the same, is all I hear from the kitchen gossip or from my partner. He don't talk much . . . studying, you know. He has an important position. Lordy, I'll be surprised if I don't lose him off to some fancy London museum, the way he's going on about it." Corky was ready to drop the cat subject. "Last I heard from him . . . and these days, he isn't talking much . . . is that the staff, and Mr. Britely, are all deeply sad; go about with long faces. Troy wonders how the manor and its occupants can go on without Sir Simon. I know it's a tragedy, but really life goes on. Don't it now?"

"Indeed it does. Perceptive of you."

Corky gave Mr. Brotherton a wide important smile. With Troy's ongoing study efforts, Corky had made it clear that each evening she intended to go down to The Bucket after her kitchen work was done for the day. Troy had nothing on his mind but memorizing every tidbit he could find about not only the statuary, paintings, and bibelots to be seen in the rooms open to the public, but also about the family and its ancestors—so many people, so many stories. He was determined to be a fount of information, and already he was able to answer most of the questions with which anyone dared challenge him. He wanted though, to be thought of as an expert; sound like an expert, look like an expert, and he began to smarten his appearance. Soon, he would say to anyone nearby, "Just ask me a question about the manor, its dwellers, its history. Go ahead, ask me." He was happy for Corky to head on off to The Bucket. She didn't drink much, she got to relax, and it left the flat quiet for his studies. She had told Troy about Mr. Brotherton who was considering writing essays about village life, and Troy understood that she felt like an expert as she provided the man with information. More power to Corky: she hadn't had many opportunities.

Before pulling all the way down the lane to the entrance, Agent Collins let Schrödinger out of the car, and by the time the agent had arrived at the front steps, the cat had already leaped ahead and up the stairs to greet Brooks. Perfect, Collins thought. It appeared exactly that the cat had merely been foraging and had decided to come in for a proper meal. Brooks said nothing about the cat, happy to see him back. He petted Schrödinger as if this were just another normal day. But when Collins greeted Brooks, did he perceive that the butler appeared less sad? A bit lighter? Knowing?

Schrödinger romped across the hall, up the grand staircase, and into the library ahead of Agent Collins, and although the days were warming, the manor's ancient stones held the cool, against which fires were kept glowing in many rooms. Thus Schrödinger knew exactly where to look for Emma. He said hello to her, received the petting he knew she wanted to bestow, and then he stretched out by the fire.

"Schrödinger, we've missed you so much," Emma said, more than pleased that the pet was warming by the fire; he was closely associated with memories of Simon. "Please don't go so far, Schrödinger; we worry about you. You must have heard Agent Collins arriving . . . so good that you came in with him."

As usual, on these visits, Agent Collins arrived just in time for a cocktail. Lady Haversham seemed a little brighter, he thought, but still that deep sadness had a permanent home within her eyes. This evening the conversation revolved around Peter and the news that he and Laura, who worked summers and holidays at the village bakery, were engaged to marry. Both were Ph.D. candidates, Laura in genetics, and Peter in computer systems. And where they would live in the future was a problem, for Peter had the responsibility of continuing as head of the estate. On Simon's death, he became the Sixth Earl of Cav Neumont. And so this topic was bandied about for a bit until there was a pause in the room while they thought of all the possibilities: could Laura and Peter someday work from the manor? Agent Collins listened to this chatter while smiling to himself that their concerns and plans would soon be disrupted. And as he waited for any new information to report to the earl, he was rewarded by that which Lady Mardling said next.

"That man we often see sitting on the green . . . he's certainly hanging around for a long time. Can he actually find pleasure by daily just sitting in our village?"

"Oh, that's Mr. Tyler Brotherton," Emma said. "He sometimes speaks to me when I take a walk up Main. He's taking a holiday . . . he's quite fond of Major."

"Well, I see him often looking across to the shop," Lady Mardling said. "He reads, but it doesn't seem that he's all that interested in his paper. He watches who comes into the shop. I wonder why. When you speak to him next, Emma, ask him whether he's looking for his missing wife. I think we get all the wives," she laughed. "Perhaps he expects she'll eventually turn up."

"I've noticed him as well," said Lady Charlotte Southway. "And Edward is curious about him . . . Mr. Brotherton, you say?"

Emma did not miss the softening in Charlotte, her look of pleasure when she mentioned Edward.

Agent Collins paid particular attention to this topic about a man who often sits on the green, who appears to read, and appears to watch who goes into New Chance. This might be of interest to Command; he must try to learn more.

In but two days, when no one was looking except possibly Brooks, Agent Collins scooped up Schrödinger and tucked him quickly into the car. Schrodinger, knowing with his wise being, what would happen, didn't complain, and straightaway settled down on the passenger seat. Brooks, with an idea about what *might* be happening, pretended not to see, and as well, didn't complain. And so it went that Lord Haversham had another two days company with his pet; good company. Schrodinger settled into his second home as if a cat expected a second home.

With each visit to The Bucket, mainly to meet Mr. Brotherton, Corky's sense of importance grew. And she became more observant about goings on at the manor, hoping to learn any morsel in which Tyler Brotherton would show interest. She was completely innocent in this effort, not at all suspecting him of subterfuge.

"Again I heard the butler and footman talking about that silly cat," she said one evening. "The footman, Hadley's his name, said the cat had appeared, and Lady Haversham was relieved. And the butler, Brooks, merely smiled. He alone seems strangely relaxed these days among all this grief. His look of despair has been replaced by a pleased look. Wonder what's on his mind . . . the only person at the manor who seems happy."

"So, you say the cat comes back, and the butler looks happy. Do you think he's happy about the cat's return?"

"He's happy enough about something."

8

A meeting was in progress at a Russian hideout: Tyler Brotherton was meeting with his handlers, Comrade Blinov and Comrade Tsarsko, the men responsible for the pipe bomb; hardened men with a new mission to determine what had happened, dead or alive, to Lord Haversham. Clearly, a memorial had been erected to the earl, and a memorial service held in the manor's chapel; the comrades had joined the attendees to witness that. But it had all happened so fast, the Russians thought. No time set aside for laboratory analysis of the remains. Short of digging up the urn they knew MI-5 had presented to Lady Haversham, the comrades had questions that needed to be answered.

With Comrade Fitzpatrick conveniently placed at New Chance to gain information, and MI-5 mole Brotherton situated on the green, and Watts watching Westminster, and commandos in hiding, they were nevertheless at a momentary standstill. Keeping left hand apart from right, they had not informed Fitzpatrick or Brotherton of each other's role: let them watch each other—the good old Russian way. Agent Brotherton was paid a large sum to report to the comrades anything he could learn about the manor's activities, or about activities at New Chance, and he had said it wasn't absolutely clear whether identifiable remains of Lord Haversham had been found. But, as well, he had heard nothing to indicate that the earl was alive. Moreover, he said, there was no DNA testing on the remains that had been distributed to families. Quite suspicious the comrades thought. And, furthermore Brotherton said, the silence on the topic among MI-5 agents was surprising.

He mentioned the manor's missing cat. "Probably not important, but one of the staff, a woman I've told you about, Corky, tells me a strange story about the manor's pet cat. The cat, a favored pet of Lord Haversham's, disappeared for two days, then suddenly reappeared for another two days, then disappeared again. Whereas, previously, this cat, free to run in and out, was known to stay inside by a fireplace."

"Ah. I can tell you more about that," said Agent Watts. "While I'm watching who arrives at MI-5 Command, I've seen a man, probably an operative, sometimes driving in or out with what appears to be an animal in the car. With my scope, I can barely see its head; it's not that clear from my position across the river. What interest would MI-5 have in an animal?"

"We need to learn more about that," said Blinov. "I know that an MI-5 agent frequently visits the manor."

"That's true," said Brotherton. "I've seen the car going up the road toward the manor."

"Anything else?"

"Yes. The woman at the bar, Corky, said there was much discussion about the missing cat. She heard it from the footman when he and the butler came down to the kitchen to eat. She said the footman was quite concerned, but the butler had nothing to say about it, and actually seemed pleased; whereas previously he had been one of the most pained."

There was a pause while the Russians sat around the long table, smoking, flicking ashes, and giving each other meaningful looks.

"Must be the same animal you've seen, Watts," said Blinov.

"Yes, I watch that gate all day until dusk; don't miss a thing. Almost overnight, they have cleaned up the explosive mess and reinstalled the checkpoint. But the operation isn't smooth yet. Cars are stopped longer now before admission. Gives me a minute to try and see what and who's in any car."

"All right. You two are doing well; keep it up. Maybe we have an indication that Lord Haversham is alive and held within MI-5. *And has visits from a cat*! That ought to be one for the books. Most men have visits from a hooker. Our guy has visits from a *cat*. Just wait until I tell headquarters that! Cross fingers that we don't get moved to desk jobs for turning looney in the field."

As the Russian comrades left the meeting they had something to laugh about—not a frequent occurrence in their line. Turning out of the room, Comrade Tsarsko held Brotherton back until the other men were out of hearing.

"Let's stir things up a bit and see what happens." His heavy Russian accent rumbled down the hallway. With dread, Brotherton waited for the order he sensed was coming. Tsarsko made certain his squinty threatening eyes, pierced Brotherton; let Brotherton feel his power. While Brotherton waited, Tsarsko stared hard at him, lit a cigarette, and then the dreaded order came: "I want that cat! Bring me that cat!"

"But Comrade Tsarsko, you need a litter box and cat food."

"Never mind all that just bring me that cat."

This posed a new problem for Brotherton for he had not been to the manor. After all it was four miles up the road from the village, and once there, he knew from surveillance photos, there was no hiding place; one would be fully exposed anywhere around the manor. Fetch a cat! He didn't know the cat's habits, or how he could capture it.

He expected Corky to be at The Bucket this evening; perhaps, without being direct, he could get a hint from her. She could be dense; still, if he asked too many questions she might become suspicious. For a minute or two he waited outside The Bucket watching people move in and out while he reviewed what he had gotten himself into: this involvement with a woman of no interest to him at all. Turncoat for money? Not really his nature when he really thought about it. Finally, he knew he had to push on and push himself into The Bucket. And there she sat.

Obviously waiting for Brotherton's arrival, Corky was turned to the door to see who was coming in. She had taken considered care to spruce up.

Ut oh, he thought, he did not want to make a relationship out of this. And did she wear false eyelashes? He thought so, real bushes, even from across the room. He would eventually have to let her down. He had begun to think that he was in the wrong occupation: he didn't want to hurt people. Or cats. He thought of leaving this work altogether. If they would let him.

"Hello, my dear, you're a sight," he said. "It's always good to see you. Might I treat you?"

She smiled broadly—teeth trying to go in all directions—and said hello. With a chubby hand done up with bright red fingernails, she patted the stool next to her for him to come sit. She sat quite elegantly on her stool, one leg crossed over the other, bouncing the upper leg, her skirt raised higher than required. She appeared to be thinning down a bit. He wanted to avoid her teasing eyes locking on to him, looking him over. His first thought was to dispel her ideas, whatever they were.

"How are your partner's studies going?" He knew from past hints that this would be a cooling topic for her. "Is he actually working now as docent?" He couldn't have cared, but he put seriousness into the question as though this were quite important.

"Yes. He works at it six days a week, but he still studies. Me thinks the information is endless, as well as difficult. Glad it isn't me. But let's not talk about him. We're not married, you know."

"Yes, I know that." He motioned for Barney to bring him the usual and while he waited, he looked around the room as though he were interested in the customers. He wanted to avoid Corky's suggestive smile and her bouncing knee. He sensed too keenly how she watched him. As well, pressing into his brain was a second thought—he had been ordered to capture the cat, and until he decided how to get out of this mess and leave his skin intact, he'd better do that. He must concentrate on finding a way to go about it. So, he had better give Corky the attention she sought. She made it easy for him.

"There's a new situation at the manor now," she said. "They've been ordered by the authorities to lock up: keep all the doors locked. The butler and footman were talking about that during lunch; talking about the difficulty. Brooks said it would take at least a half-hour to cover all the doors, and days to cover the windows, but if it kept the family safer . . . from he didn't know what . . . that's what they would do."

"My word. I wonder what has happened . . . what they are expecting to happen?"

"You got me, but after they ate, Brooks took down the map of the manor and went off to make two copies. They would need maps to be sure no door or French window was missed. Then while I sat over my coffee, he came back with a copy for Hadley. Brooks was to take the manor's south wing and Hadley the north."

"And how does the cat get out then?" This might be an opportunity to get some of the information he needed.

"Oh, that's not a problem, he has a little swinging trap door at the rear of the back hallway, off the kitchen. He knows to go to that pet door."

45

"And you say the cat comes and goes."

"Yup. Most strange. When his lordship was alive, Schrofer, or whatever the thing's name is, was purely a house cat, stayed around, stepping out only to do his business. At least this is what I hear in the kitchen. I just saw him today though, so he has decided to be at the manor for a while."

"Ah. Smart cat." Agent Brotherton felt some relief. Perhaps his job would not be as difficult as he feared. He couldn't cross Comrade Tsarsko; the man was a monster. He wondered, if he should be lucky enough to find the beast, how could he carry him back. That night he asked at the inn whether it might be possible to borrow, or hire, one of their golf carts. He had noticed that they had quiet battery-operated golf carts to help with maintenance around the inn, and however he was to do this, he had to proceed with absolute quiet. Of course, they said. Certainly.

Agent Brotherton waited until dark to drive the cart up the lane to the manor. This was the strangest of any of his assignments, and he was not sure how to proceed, but he would wait around the rear of the manor near the back kitchen door. If he could find it. And he had had the foresight to buy a can of tuna, the best kind. It took about thirty minutes to drive the cart from The Meridian to the manor's rear, where he found a place to sit on a wall in a dark area. He opened the can of tuna and trying to make himself as comfortable as possible, he waited.

His wait was short, for as soon as the tuna's strong fishy smell, wafted across the kitchen courtyard, through the cracks in the ancient windows, up the stairs and throughout the manor—especially the library where Schrödinger, relaxed before the fire—to remind him of a treasure he rarely had, he suddenly sprang up to seek out this treasure. The aroma led Schrödinger down stairs, across hallways, and into the kitchen, then eventually to the cat door from where the strongest odor of tuna emanated. It took him no effort at all to find Agent Brotherton sitting on a wall in the dark. When the agent heard Schrödinger spring out the cat door, he placed the can of tuna on the ground by his feet. Thinking it extremely unfair to immediately pick up Schrödinger, he allowed the cat to feast, then sensing the feline belly to be full, he picked him up, and carried him struggling and yelling around toward the cart. He held the cat as gently as he could; he actually liked cats and felt sorry for it. He held it as lovingly as possible, and Schrödinger, by now used to being moved around, settled down until they reached the cart. On its rear, the cart had a lidded contraption into which Brotherton stowed Schrödinger, who, deciding this was too much to endure, set up a wail.

"Don't worry, mate," Brotherton called back. "You're safe and will have a nice room to stay in tonight." Safe?—safe after being turned over to Comrade Tsarsko? He began to worry about the cruel side of Tsarsko. What would Tsarsko do with the cat after he had satisfied his curiosity? On the dark drive to the inn, Brotherton thought about the nice cat that had done no harm. Could he actually turn the creature over to Tsarsko? What else could he do? Borrow the inn's cart again and take the cat back? What would he say to Tsarsko? That man expected nothing short of performance. And although, except for the cat's comings and goings, he had yet to pass information to the Russians, they were paying him a fortune to perform as told. And he was growing used to the money. He had to give this serious thought.

At the inn he parked the cart and took Schrödinger inside. The concierge stared hard at the guest coming in with a cat; cats were allowed, but only for an extra fee.

"Don't worry," Brotherton said, making an effort to hide Schrödinger as he hurried past the front desk. "He's here only until tomorrow. I'll settle up with you when I check out." He was grateful that the employee merely stared, said nothing. But, once in the room, he realized he had a new problem: yes, he could supply plenty of tuna going into the cat, but what about tuna coming out? And he was more convinced that he couldn't turn the nice creature over to Tsarsko. This was a serious problem; he was about to be in deep trouble.

He was tired now. He would think more clearly in the morning. He turned into bed. Schrödinger seemed at peace with arrangements and settled in on top of the covers beside this man, who had so far treated him well, and must be taking him to his best friend.

In the morning, Brotherton realized he had no time to return the cat back to the manor. And anyway he could hardly do that in the morning. Of course, he could just put the cat out somewhere, but the manor was probably four or five miles from the inn, and he liked the creature and wanted to see him safely back with his family. His most immediate problem was that he had to shower, dress, and drive to London for an early meeting with MI-5. He couldn't miss that without their investigating. Then he had a brilliant idea: he could take Schrofer, or whatever his name was, with him. With security at MI-5 as it was, with man-traps preventing coming-and-going without retinae recognition, turned loose—the cat would actually be safe within MI-5's Command. And should they have Lord Haversham in secure hiding, that over-smart feline would find him.

Carrying Schrödinger, Brotherton entered the meeting. All eyes turned to stare at him. "Sorry, gentleman, I had to bring a cat with me, and before coming in, I had to let him relieve himself in our back garden. I'm delivering him to a friend." This did draw strange looks from the agents seated around the table, but it guaranteed for Brotherton that should Schrödinger not find Haversham, and instead ran loose around headquarters, there would be enough agents aware of the situation to know to return the cat to himself. Success, he felt. A strange situation, but then most of MI-5's concerns were strange. And if the cat did not find Lord Haversham, he could take a night to return it to the manor. He would *not* be giving it to Comrade Tsarsko. After dark, in his office at Command, he opened the door to the hallway and said to Schrödinger, "Go to it mate. Best of luck to you." And he shut the door closing the cat out in the hallway.

He went to sleep that night feeling the peace that for a while had been lost to him. He had made a decision and knew that the cat, whether or not he found Haversham, would be safe.

Indeed, Lord Haversham was there, and it wasn't long before Schrödinger knew it to be so. Detecting that his master was on another floor, the cat picked the correct staircase and raced up.

Lord Haversham wasn't sleeping well: suffering depression for his colleagues who had been killed, worried about Emma, knowing her pain. Worries about how all this would turn out kept him tossing into the night. Every night. His only comforts were the visits allowed with his cat. And if he could believe his ears, Schrödinger was meowing outside his door to be let in. Surely this was his own tiredness, for the cat was not with him now. Schrödinger had been carried back to the manor for a few days so that Emma and everyone else at the manor would not worry about him. Schrödinger was definitely at the manor now, he was certain. Still he could hear those meows. Simon wearily tossed and turned trying harder to sleep, but those meows grew louder and more persistent. Finally Simon had to sit up in bed; he *heard* meows! He went to the door and opened it to see a flash of orange cat rush in, a flurry of cat hair rushing past him. He turned around in shock to see Schrödinger waiting on the bed, washing a paw, purring, contented as ever to be with Simon again, acting as though nothing unusual had happened. Simon petted the cat and climbed under the covers. So tired. He would not wonder tonight where Schrödinger had been. Time for that puzzle in the morning when he would ask Agent Collins whether he knew anything about it; that chap had more cats up his sleeve.

When the cat did not turn up, and no one at Command said anything about seeing a cat loose in the building, Brotherton still had at least two new problems. For one, he had to figure out what to tell Tsarsko, and two, he didn't think so, but Comrade Watts at Tsarsko's meeting may have learned more precisely that Lord Haversham, if he were hidden there, had visits from a cat. But this was of lesser importance, he thought, for he was ready to turn in his resignation, he wasn't cut out for espionage. He had had some infantile idea about the excitement of espionage, the money, and eventually retiring to the Canary Islands. His guilt reminded him about the money the Russians had paid him, and he was quite ready, decided in fact, to return it. Or, if that were impossible, to donate it to an orphanage, or something: get rid of it. But first, of vital importance was the story he had to give Tsarsko, who would have his head.

"Lost! You've lost the cat!" Comrade Tsarsko demanded of Agent Brotherton. "What the hell do you mean by that?" He exploded in Russian, carefully but instantly choosing impactful Russian swears. Brotherton knew enough Russian to be fully aware of the danger.

"Yes. Lost. He escaped from the golf cart when I was bringing him from the manor," a convenient and handy lie. Tsarsko's eyes spit fire! Brotherton rushed to dampen the flames: "Without a key, I couldn't lock the back compartment where I had tucked him." This wasn't the only message Brotherton had to give Comrade Tsarsko. He dreaded it, but he had decided on a way to get out of service to the Russians. "And Comrade Tsarsko, please permit me to say . . . I cannot be any further use to you as I've been dismissed from MI-5 for lack of performance." This wasn't yet true, but he knew it soon would be.

Tsarsko was about to order, *you find that cat*, but instead Tsarsko glared at Brotherton with deepest anger. Around the table, the other comrades, trying not to breathe, were well aware that Tsarsko's anger could reach out to each of them in some dreadful way.

"Then you are correct. You are no longer of use to me!" The fire in Tsarsko's eyes seemed to have the heat to ignite the room. Still a chill swept through Brotherton.

"Right, Comrade. I completely understand."

"Go! Leave now. You'll be lucky if we don't terminate you."

But Tyler Brotherton had not yet worked on something of any importance to Tsarsko. He felt that having no inside information about the Russians' operation, he was reasonably safe. He didn't even know where they held meetings, for it continually changed. They would let him go. He had acquired no information about their operations that MI-5 didn't already know. It would be a waste of resources to extinguish him.

"Grant, I ask you, where did my cat come from?"

Agent Collins had arrived with a new supply of cat litter for Schrödinger's box, and a bag full of cat cereal and cans of cat food. Sometimes staff at Command kidded Collins about running a kennel in the building. He had no answer for Simon. "You say late at night you heard him meowing outside your door?"

"Precisely."

"He was loose in the hallway?"

"Right."

"I wonder what the guard thought."

"Probably asleep."

"Ah! I wonder whether he took the bus or the train. Aren't you a mystery, Schrödinger! I knew you were special." Agent Collins laughed; whatever was the answer, it was amusing. *Amusing* wasn't exactly the description, he mused. Had he lost his senses? Hadn't he delivered Schrödinger to the manor!

9

Agent Brotherton submitted his resignation to MI-5. He told them he was unfit for the job; was too soft; had no stomach for it. They didn't know the real reason, but had to take his word. It was not wise to try to keep an agent who was reluctant to do the work. They had to think about what vital and secret information he carried with him, and it wasn't much to get excited about they decided, and they let him go. His only assignment had been to keep an eye on New Chance; determine whether any unlikely strangers had an interest in the shop. He had mentioned to them the man who seemed to work there on certain days, and Command was in the process of learning who the man was. The fact that Lord Haversham was held in strict security was known to only a few, and not to Brotherton. However, since the cat had not shown up, was not mentioned, and apparently not seen, Brotherton had a good idea that they held Haversham hidden away in a safe room. He felt good about that— suspected that the cat had found the earl.

Meanwhile, he had enough money to keep his room at The Meridian Inn in Cav Neumont Village, and wasn't ready to give that up. He needed peace from worry, and would sit again on the bench in the village and read. He needed a pause in which to think about his next employment. He had no intention to meet Corky again at The Bucket Arms. Still, he wanted to enjoy a quiet ale there in the evenings. This could be rather sticky, so instead, for a few nights he would have that drink and a meal at The Meridian. It was more expensive and not as relaxed as The Bucket but the food was excellent. Altogether a soft life, so far.

"That man is out there again," said Edward Fitzpatrick. Working alongside Lady Charlotte Southway at New Chance, he took a few slow minutes from helping her, to watch passers-by.

"Yes, a Mr. Brotherton. He missed a few days, though," Charlotte said. "And he doesn't watch us, as we used to think. Doesn't seem to have an interest in who comes and goes from here. For whatever reason, if the weather's fine he either walks or sits and reads. And writes. He seems to be writing in a journal." She continued to iron shirts that she had taken from the back room, then she would hand them to Edward to hang. "I've asked Emma, when she comes in from walking Major, if she knows what the man is about, for I've noticed that on occasion she stops to have a word with him. She says he's unemployed, and taking a holiday before job hunting."

Unemployed? Hmm, Edward wondered, the man didn't look familiar, and Tsarsko hadn't seemed to find him of interest; he could let it go.

10

When Tyler Brotherton became scarce, no longer holding down a seat at The Bucket Arms Tavern, Corky tired of looking for him. And although he had made no promises to her, he had fed her expectations and she did miss him. Men were interesting to her; mainly handsome men who exuded a certain undercurrent of sexual tension about them—at least in her mind. Troy had become dull, not one she enjoyed as much these days. He didn't go on that she was pretty, or that she was sexy, alluring, and so on. Didn't gaze at her; gaze at what she had to offer. Without actually voicing this to herself, she felt it. She continued to come in from work, freshen up, say bye to Troy, always pouring over his books, say she would be back later, and head on off to The Bucket. She would sit there alone, speak a bit to Barney, play with her dinner, and hope Tyler would come in. Barney said he hadn't seen him at all lately, putting paid to her flirtatious hopes. She would go home disappointed, and Troy would greet her, and want to talk about his studies, she would respond sourly that she really wasn't in a mood to hear it.

What was bothering her, Troy wondered. Previously she had always come in chatty and happy. He would study a bit more, then go to bed alone, while she sat up stewing about something. He couldn't help her. Especially when she had nothing to say. He had his work that every day grew more valuable to him. He had even seen Emma, Lady Haversham, stop by to admire his docere technique for the public. He knew that she stopped to listen to his little speeches. And to think—he had once found those lovely and impressive statues to be of interest only if they wore a teddy and could wink at him. His heart went out to Lady Haversham, and in her grief and sadness, he felt important to be helping at the manor. He went to sleep pleased that he was learning something important to many people. Then his last thoughts before dropping off the cliff of sleep were the same as everyone else's—about his lordship. He also missed him. When for the twenty years that Troy was the earl's groundsman, his lordship had always been kind and fair; had made it clear that he valued his work. Could Lord Haversham but see him now. Strange thing about his lordship's pet cat, he thought; the staff talks about it around the dinner table. Whereas the cat used to sit on his tower in the dining room, or in the breakfast room next to Lord Haversham, now it goes and comes, usually two days at a time.

11

Although Emma never felt genuine happiness, when she felt herself sinking into despair, she would rally enough to keep working at New Chance where her time and attention were truly needed. And there were the good people who also rallied around to help—her volunteers: Lady Mardling, Lady Southway, Hannah, Lady Claire (the former Lady Haversham), and now even Edward. They had all made the shop a success; it was one of the biggest draws in the county. On the days when Emma worked at the shop, Major would accompany her. Together they would walk the four miles from the manor to the village, or if weather didn't allow, either Hadley would drive them over, or Emma would drive, and sometimes she would tuck Major beside her in one of the manor's golf carts. Then, during the workday, she would find a few occasions to take Major for a walk along the village green. Walking Major gave Emma time to think about how things had turned out now that Simon was gone. In the midst of her loss she felt love all around her, and for which she was grateful. *The quality of mercy.*

It was a lovely time to walk up Main; Emma had grown to love this village that in this time of grief had a soothing effect; helped her to work through her thoughts and concerns. She was concerned that Count Bianco, who lived in London, might take Lady Mardling permanently away from the village. The shop needed Aggie, but she herself needed Aggie—it would be hard to lose someone who had been close to Simon—keeping his memory fresh. Emma's thoughts now moved to Laura and Peter, Simon's adopted son. They were to be married. It would fall to Peter in the main to be responsible for the estate. Peter treasured the manor and it's gardens, orchards, and fields; Emma knew that. But with his and Laura's university degrees, where would life take them? Of course, John Britely, with Hannah's help, directly managed the estate, and quite well he did; cherished the manor and grounds as much as Simon had. So that was a good thing about which Emma could relax. What other concerns would arrive, she wondered.

Major led Emma over to a bench where an enormous elm provided coolness from the sun. It had been quite strong the past few days as if putting forth a placeholder. It did feel good to sit in the shade for a while, before going back to help at the shop. With so many on holiday, shop sales could be handled by two, or even one person, and Emma knew she didn't have to hurry across; she could see the shop from where she sat. Lady Southway was working there today. Later on Emma would give her a break, letting her walk Major should she wish.

Today their new friend, Edward came in to join Charlotte. He had become almost like family, and perhaps, seeing that he was right fond of Charlotte, he might indeed become family, for Emma had always thought of Charlotte that way. He was there because of Charlotte, Emma thought. That could become a new worry—would he soon take Charlotte to live in Craig-on-Wold, take her away from Emma and the shop? In her mind, Emma wanted to move all of them to Cav Neumont. Not just because of needing them to volunteer at New Chance, but because she had grown to love them all so much, and how could she bear to lose them?

Now that man, Mr. Brotherton, approached. He tipped his hat, and with a smile warmer than he had shown before, said hello and asked whether he might join her. For some reason, though at first he had seemed off, stiff, he now seemed relaxed, and Emma welcomed his company. He said he was still staying at The Meridian. They talked for a while about things simple and every day. The shade felt good and they both seemed in no hurry. He petted Major.

"Mr. Brotherton, Major has taken to you."

"Ah, yes, he's the kind of pet one easily loves. But, please call me Tyler. Major calls me Tyler, don't you my friend?" Brotherton knew almost everything: he knew that it was likely that Lord Simon Haversham, the man this woman grieved for, was still alive and in safe hiding; he knew that it was likely that the pet cat, which he had whisked away, then turned loose at Command Headquarters, was with Haversham. Brotherton wasn't certain, but according to what he had heard at Tsarsko's meeting, someone carted that cat back and forth, probably so the earl had company and Lady Emma Haversham had no excessive worry about the cat's whereabouts. Someone cared a great deal about bestowing an unusual bit of happiness where possible. But, he couldn't mention any of this to the woman sitting beside him. He was uncertain about everything, except that he had been absolutely positive that he could not deliver the cat to Comrade Tsarsko. He had given up his career in MI-5, because of a mistake he had made and hoped to correct, and because he could not work as a mole for the Russians and for Comrade Tsarsko.

"Where do you live when you're not on holiday?" Emma asked.

"I've been leasing a flat in London, but as I'm changing my employment, I'll probably be moving."

"What *is* your background, if I might ask?" Impertinent, but she might hear of something relevant and be of use to him.

"Security. I'm a specialist in keeping people and firms safe. Safe and secure. I can work for a business, or for an individual. I'll just have to see what comes up. That will decide for me where to move, should I need to."

Emma felt comfortable with Tyler, and in the next few days, they often met on that bench, always when Emma walked Major. One day she said, "I suppose you are familiar with our tragedy. And, since the assassins have not been captured, although I am told that their locations are known and they will soon be captured, we at the manor have been told by MI-5 to lock every entrance." It was impossible for her to say, *they were never locked before Lord Haversham's life ended.* "That has changed our coming and going. Talk about security, I guess we've needed some at the manor. Perhaps we could hire you to come check us out," she said kind of as an afterthought. "Agent Collins from MI-5 drops in briefly, but he's not a security specialist."

Tyler Brotherton's brow hunched up at this information. His background had indeed been in security; that was true. If needed to, he could wire every window and door to an alarm, as well as to a camera, and in a hidden manner. He was an expert at keeping both installations and individuals secure from threats, real or perceived. Was this a signal that he might find work right here in Cav Neumont? He didn't want to push though he would welcome the opportunity. And Collins? He had heard of Agent Collins. What if Collins vetted him and learned that he is an MI-5 has-been? What would that recognition do to him? He wouldn't run. After all, he didn't wash out, he quit. He examined his past and found nothing absolutely to regret. So far no one knew he had been a mole, and should they find out, they would not be able to find any act he had committed against England, for there had been none. He had quit in time. And he had refused to hand over the Haversham pet cat. He had become, after all, a man of honor. Thank the powers-that-be for that. *It droppeth like the gentle rain on all below.*

"It's up to our estate manager, Mr. John Britely to hire for the manor," Emma said. "Think about this and should you be interested in looking into the position, I'll introduce you to him. Let's talk again in a few days." She stood, held out her hand, shook hands with Mr. Brotherton, said goodbye, and walked with Major across to the shop.

Tyler Brotherton watched them cross the street. A lovely woman, he thought. Her sadness had not caused her to lose her soft looks, her commanding presence, or her splendid long dark hair onto which he enjoyed seeing the sun shine. He had much to think about. It would be too good to be true that he could help the people the terrorists had hurt. He wouldn't waste time hoping. Not today, but tomorrow, he might stop in to New Chance, see what it was all about. There was no reason for him not to do so.

Lady Southway stopped ironing to stare at the man. Edward Fitzpatrick held up, as though frozen, the shirt he was about to hang. While they were face to face with the mysterious man, Emma made the introductions around as though the man were a best friend.

"I asked Mr. Brotherton to come in for tea. He's on holiday and staying at The Meridian."

"Oh, yes, tea. Do have a cup, Mr. Brotherton," said Lady Southway, and she led him to the back room where Major had made himself comfortable under the tea table. She watched while Mr. Brotherton knelt to pet Major. Interesting, she thought, for she had noticed that the dog was wary of Edward—he would give out the faintest of snarls when Edward reached to pet him, and yet Major was most amenable when Mr. Brotherton gave him a rub. And

Tyler Brotherton seemed happy to have the dog close by, as though the dog were company in his, what seemed to be, bleak life.

Customers came in and began to browse through the racks of dresses.

"Am I apt to be in the way here," Tyler Brotherton asked, an uncertain look taking over his face.

"Not at all, we planned plenty of room for tea. Don't worry if a customer wants to try on something . . . we have the back room for that." Emma felt good inviting him in; he had appeared to be somewhat lost.

As he sat, occasionally petting Major under the table, he pondered what to do with the money he had been paid for being an MI-5 mole for the Russians. His turning for them, though brief, felt disgusting to him now. At the time, he had been swayed by the money, thought he needed it, and it had been his fear for the welfare of a cat that taught him he couldn't do the job. Just the small act of finding a certain cat and turning it over to Tsarsko, then not knowing what would be the cat's uncertain fate, had taught him this. He might remain unemployed for a while but he was thankful that he had quit in time. All because of a cat with an odd, un-rememorable, name. Why did Mr. Fitzpatrick stare at him so conspicuously?

That evening while Emma, Hannah and John Britely enjoyed cocktails, Emma thought to mention Mr. Brotherton. They had quite a few guests this night, as often happened, everyone wanting to keep Emma distracted, a little happier if possible. Also in attendance were Lady Mardling and Count Bianco. As well, Lady Charlotte Southway had invited Edward Fitzpatrick, and Peter and Laura were there. Peter had picked up Laura at the bakery and would be driving her home after dinner. Companionable gossip circled about; only Emma seemed alone and lost. Agent Grant Collins, had stopped in this evening. He would never stay for dinner though, as his wife waited dinner for him. Light gossip was the norm and spread itself around the group as they waited for the call to dinner.

"The man I introduced to you today, Mr. Tyler Brotherton," Emma said to Lady Mardling, "is the same man we've seen so often sitting on the bench across the street. I've told you about him, he's on holiday and staying at The Meridian." She looked around, for she knew that most of the others knew about the man as well.

"Ah yes. The man Major takes to so." said Lady Southway.

"Exactly. Occasionally he has sat with me when Major and I stopped to rest a few minutes in the shade. He's quite affable. Turns out that he's looking for a new position; taking this holiday to think it over." She looked at John Britely. "His specialty, John, is security; security for corporations, buildings, and even individuals."

John listened to her intently.

"He has years of experience in that field. Do we . . . now that our government's security sgency has ordered us to lock the manor's doors . . . ," she gave a nod to Agent Collins, "need to think further about security?"

"It wouldn't hurt," Agent Collins said. "You might at least talk to him, Mr. Britely. See what he has to offer. Perhaps a walk around with him would be beneficial. Get his advice about alarms."

Edward's ears picked up. This was information to pass on to Tsarsko.

"But we don't know him at all," John said. "It's always been our policy to deal only with those whom we know well."

"I don't know the man, haven't seen him, so I can't say anything about him at this point; however, I could work him up . . . draw down his history," said Agent Collins.

"Please do," Emma said. "If you don't mind. He's always around, as I said, and for the first time came into the shop today."

A general discussion ensued on the topic of what security for the manor might entail. Then Brooks announced dinner and the group moved through to the dining room. Though Simon wasn't there, Emma's heart felt lighter with the company of her friends and family. She loved them all.

Before they went in, Agent Collins, on leaving, said that he would return with information about Mr. Tyler Brotherton. And within the next few days when he did, his news was not good. Although he had *not* learned about Brotherton's deception as a mole, he had learned that the man had been an agent for MI-5, and recently had given notice saying he couldn't handle the work. *Couldn't handle the work*! What kind of recommendation was that for a person to be considered as a security expert for the manor? Still, Brotherton did have a long career in security, and no mishap had occurred on his record. His references were excellent. Collins told John Britely what he learned about Tyler Brotherton; now it was his and Lady Emma's decision.

Tyler avoided the days when he thought Edward Fitzpatrick would be there—the man did stare at him so. And as well, Tyler had a wary sense about the man who claimed to be a science journalist. Tyler subscribed to a science magazine, and he had not heard of this Mr. Fitzpatrick. Still, as he was only a bystander, it was uncalled for to serve up questions. On any other day, Tyler felt comfortable now dropping into New Chance for tea, and a word with Lady Haversham. Formerly he had his tea behind the bakery, but it was rather solitary back there, and New Chance was usually jumping with activity. As well, their tea table was set just far enough back that he could relax there out of the way of shoppers.

In between looking out the back window at starlings darting about a pond, he could read and pet Major, have his tea and leave after putting a sizable cash donation into the box meant for the parish. He was slowly dispersing that which he had received from the Russians.

He admired the volunteers at New Chance. He had met them all: Lady Mardling, Lady Southway, and Hannah, and during these days, he witnessed the family's and friends' sadness. Lady Emma's mouth, so pretty, could sometimes be caught turning down at the corners. No one laughed, or at least seldom laughed. Tyler Brotherton was well aware that they believed they had lost Lord Haversham in the explosion; that they would never again feel really happy or joyous about something. Or would they? Not much was certain.

12

Agent Grant Collins arrived rolling in a trolley covered with Simon's breakfast. "Good morning, sir. Mind if I join you?" Collins said.

Straight away, Simon understood that it wasn't in fact to be considered a question, for Grant spread dishes about then took a seat at the table. Then he lifted his hand toward Simon's chair and looked at Simon as if to say, Your presence at table, sir.

"Right. I see, Grant, that you don't need an invitation. Go right ahead and help yourself whilst I decide whether *you* may join *me*." He gave the agent one of his rare smiles. "You look cheerful this morning. I can tell by your unusual smirk that something's improved."

Agent Collins held back his answer. He felt the power of the news he had to give his lordship. Let him wallow in a friendly stew for a minute while he served his plate. "Go ahead and start, sir. I'm waiting for you. I think you're growing lazy."

"Indeed I am," Simon said, while taking a seat opposite Agent Collins. "I want out of this place. I'm in jail without having committed a crime. What are you withholding behind your smirk?"

Agent Collins took his time thinking how to put it. He poured their coffees. "Two of the three men have been captured."

With these words Simon jerked up to attention. He stared hard at Agent Collins while he waited for whatever the man had to say next. Details. He waited for details.

"The worst of the lot, the leader, a well-trained assassin, Stepan Portnov, is still at large. He has surrounded himself with women and children such that, not wanting to incur collateral damage, our commandos, have not been able to take him yet. He's been spotted leaving what he thought was a safehouse, carrying a young child. That threw us, but next time, we're ready for him . . . and the child."

For a moment, it appeared that Simon wouldn't be able to eat; he could only think that he was two-thirds of the way home. He stared at Agent Collins. Then examining his plate, he impaled a sausage; it seemed to take less effort now to cut off a piece. He suddenly felt new energy coursing through his soul. He could see a vision of Emma coming closer. He began to eat. Perhaps things were looking up.

"You need to get him before he is able to bring in more men." Simon took a bite and, looking down at his plate, chewed slowly, as though the effort of thinking over all the angles had drained his remaining energy.

Agent Collins was nodding agreement. He yearned to tell Simon that he would be going home in a day or two, but it was too early yet to take that risk; get the man's expectations up, in the face of possible failure.

"I want to go home. I'm in pain. Emma's in pain. Peter's in pain. Even my manager, John is in pain. My valet, Pearce. I know the manor is in good hands, but I need to know that first-hand. Need to be with my precious Emma. I must go home."

"Hold on a bit. It's being discussed, and if they deem it possible, that we'll be able to keep you safe . . . and just how that will be accomplished . . . you'll be taken home."

"Right. I understand," Simon said. "Someone erroneously thinks that I know the most about putting pressure on Russia. That I single-handedly can block all world trade with Russia; leave them even without water, as it were. Not true, of course, but it became known that I headed up that committee."

"And the manor must be completely secure, that is, as much as anything can be," Agent Collins urged his caution. "They thought Westminster was safe, and look what happened. Now, they've set up temporary check points around it. Nothing gets near without being scanned. It's tied up the city's traffic such that more people have taken to bicycles and those are stopped as well. Your days of leaving the manor completely open are over."

"The manor has a rather complete security system," Simon argued.

"So I've heard. And no one uses it . . . I've also heard.

"We can tighten up on that; though it will be hard for the staff . . . you know the kitchen and service people come and go throughout the day by way of the rear kitchen entrance."

"And then there's the feeling for Lady Haversham's shock," Agent Collins wanted to press on. His eyes held meaning that Simon understood. The shock of learning that he was still alive could be as great as the shock of learning he had been killed.

"I know she will be up for it," Simon said. "She's not inclined to hysterics. She will be overcome, as well as relieved though, for she and I have become as close as twins in the womb."

Agent Collins finished his coffee, and left with the encouraging words for Simon, that Command would shortly let him know the next move.

The following day, Agent Collins again arrived to join the earl for breakfast. And while Collins spread the dishes around, Simon took a seat at the table and looked at him expectantly, boring his eyes into the agent's soul almost. Collins took his seat and began filling his plate.

"Ah, sir, this looks almost as good as the news I have for you," he said. "It's been decided . . . that is, some think, sir . . . that even though one of the assassins is still free, that first bringing Lady Haversham here to meet you will be best. Until they let you leave, that is. Let the two of you have time alone while she adjusts to the shock and becomes acquainted with the seriousness of our responsibility. Her visit will serve a dual purpose as well, sir, for Command will meet with her to advise her how caution and procedures must be observed. Then, the next day the two of you may leave together. Later Command will hold the same meeting for Cav Neumont Manor staff."

On hearing these words Simon had become transfixed, color draining from his face.

"They're discussing bringing Lady Haversham in to you by helicopter. As you know, there's a heliport on the roof. And though it's no doubt watched by those who would hurt us, helicopters are arriving and leaving every day. Lady Haversham's will just be one more of the many. And we'll see that she won't be easily recognizable."

Lord Haversham, with the worry over this news, and the worry for trying to imagine all details, kept twisting his napkin as he gave slight nods with each of the agent's points.

"Then the two of you can leave together, by helicopter," Agent Collins repeated while looking for relief on the earl's face. "They think no one can be watching the manor at close range due to its seclusion. You should be safe when you arrive there; keeping in mind that one of the Russian terrorists is still at large. But, as I said, we have eyes on him." He reached down to pet Schrödinger.

"Tonight I'll take your cat with me to the manor so he won't become an issue getting to the chopper. It would terrify him, I think."

Simon's face bore a mixture of shock, relief, and concern as he tried to focus on this news, these challenges, these joys. Schrödinger. His thoughts came down to settle on his cat. "Certainly, we cannot expect my faithful friend to tolerate a helicopter. Thank you, Grant, on Schrödinger's behalf for your forethought."

"I asked whether Command had an interest in interviewing Schrödinger for a position, but despite his stealth talents, they said no. They doubt he would qualify as an MI-5 operative; for, as you know, we are the best, and the well-known fact that we silently creep in on cat feet . . . that's just a metaphor, sir," he nodded, straight faced, with assurance.

There was a long pause. Agent Collins watched as his bit of humor, along with the news they had discussed, began slowly to lighten the earl's frown. Simon's entire demeanor seemed to lift.

"I must leave now," Collins said. "I'll return as soon as I know more." Folding his napkin onto the tray, he said goodbye for now, and wheeled out the trolley.

Lord Haversham feared his heart would beat out of control with happiness. How much more could it take? Emma! He might soon be with Emma! And Peter! And the manor and everyone else there. He had thought about all of his family and friends until his mind had grooves labelled for each. He longed for his old habits, his own bed with Emma, the daily chores and cares, the small unimportant details, the goings-on of life. He was restless that night; he could not stop thinking about Emma's learning the truth, the astounding blow for her.

13

Agent Collins arrived at Cav Neumont, and, as usual, let Schrödinger out of the car before making the final turn to the manor. And now Brooks showed him into the study where Emma sat writing.

"Good evening Lady Haversham."

Emma held out her hand to him. Always pleasant, he had somehow been a bearer of hope. She didn't understand this, for Simon was gone; how could there be hope? Still Agent Collins was always welcome; he seemed to arrive encircled with hope. He held her hand briefly, then pulled a chair up close to her.

"Brooks, would you kindly mix a martini for Agent Collins?" She had learned that most nights when he visited, he preferred a sherry, but when he arrived looking particularly tense, he wanted a martini. He had called ahead to ask whether this evening he could speak to her alone.

Having learned to trust MI-5 and its agents, and especially Agent Collins, Emma wasn't concerned about what he had to say, and expected it to be news about the threats they still faced. However, she found that she was hardly prepared for what he had to relate.

"Lady Haversham, please be ready for astounding . . . shocking . . . news. I have lived with great expectations for this moment, and now it's upon me."

Emma looked frightened.

"I'm eager to tell you . . . have been for what seems an endless expanse of time . . . that Lord Haversham is alive and well and desperate to get to you." He waited while she rejected information she knew couldn't be true. He understood that his sentence hung in some kind of never-never-land unable to be absorbed.

Emma couldn't speak. This news must be a cruel joke. What was Collins up to? She had buried Simon's remains, held a memorial for him, had grieved beyond human capacity for losing him. Yet, she had strangely felt his life—felt it around her, and had many times wondered what that was about.

As she did not speak, or make any gesture, Agent Collins continued, struggling to make sense of it for her. "Lord Haversham has been held in a highly secured suite in London at MI-5 Command. It was deemed best, absolutely, to keep his existence a total secret. I think that fewer than a half-dozen agents know of his presence there. He wasn't in the explosion, and knowing that he might still be a target should the terrorists learn of his survival, Command felt they must withhold the fact of his survival even from you, for we knew you were being watched. Your shop was being watched. It may sound like a cruel joke, but had you known Lord Haversham survived the bomb, you would, in some way, some innocent way, revealed it." Agent Collins rushed on, unsure of Lady Haversham's steadiness. He wanted to assure her, but it was not easy to find the safest way.

"At first when Sir Simon was whisked away to safety, there was much discussion about how to proceed. And it was finally decided to keep his survival secret until the terrorists were captured. Extremely cruel for all concerned . . . and you may be sure . . . there has been much thrashing about in Command for the best approach. Regardless, we knew we would bring the two of you together the instant we could keep you safe. As safe as possible." Emma looked ready to faint. He rushed on hoping to support her with a wall of assurance. "So it was deemed critically important . . . imperative for his lordship's safety to let no one know." He saw that her eyes were moist, her hands were shaking, her mouth trembled.

She thought her heart would leave her chest, it jumped about so. Dozens of thoughts both strange and wonderful came to her. Now she knew why she had heard *The Holberg* briefly on that disconnected phone call; why she had continually had the strange feeling that Simon was still alive somewhere, why Lady Joan always appeared to be pleased. And even lately why Brooks seemed more relaxed—less sad. He must have had clues somehow that Simon was alive.

Agent Collins waited, unsure of what to say next. Then wanting to interject a light note, he said, "We thought it safe to let your cat in on the secret, and I have been carrying him back and forth to give Sir Simon a bit of company. Now you know why you couldn't find him on occasion."

Emma listened, but only half heard. Schrödinger? Her head couldn't stick there and would come back to Simon. "When can I go to my husband? Does he know that I know? When can he come home?" she urged, the plaintive question frowning her face.

"Not yet, but headquarters is thinking about letting him return. He knows that I'm to tell you. This change of policy is only because two of the terrorists have been captured. The third's location is known, and soon he will go down. Thus, they've thought that Lord Haversham may safely come home, although as you know, they've requested additional security for the manor. However, while he's safely tucked away, we thought it best to come for you; take you to him." Agent Collins wanted so much to blot the tears forming in her eyes.

"Oh, yes. Please. When?" She almost wailed.

"I believe it's to be right away, perhaps tomorrow, if you can."

"If I can! I'm ready to go right now. Can I call him?"

"I'm so sorry, Lady Haversham, but I must say no. After we caught him ringing you, of course we couldn't trust him not to contact you, and his phone was removed." He couldn't bear to say, after *I* caught him ringing you, for Collins felt that responsibility too keenly. "Command insists on no phone transmission. It was all we could do to keep Sir Simon there, and daily we had to remind him of the threats to his life, and even possibly to yours. That was the only way we could deal with his anger. Had the terrorists, Blinov or Portnov, thought you knew Lord Haversham was alive, your life would have been in danger."

Agent Collins stood to leave. "I'll ring you the first thing tomorrow to give you the details. I think a helicopter will come for you. Goodnight Lady Haversham. It will be hard for you to sleep tonight." He left, his martini barely touched, his excitement over his duty pushing him out. This was almost more than he could calmly withstand.

In fact, Emma did not sleep all night. Instead, she wandered about the manor. Now, she could let the tears flow. Simon! She would be with Simon again! He was alive! How could that be? An incredible thought; was it real? Simon! Poor love, he had to go through his days knowing that she grieved horribly for him. Then finally, at four o-clock in the morning she rested her head on her pillow and slept, but not before seeing Lady Joan standing by the bed with that look that said, *I told you so,* or at least, *I tried to tell you so.*

14

In the morning, Emma had scant time to know what she was about. Agent Collins had rung on her bedside mobile and said to be ready in an hour for the helicopter to land in the front circle. Do not dress up; if she could, wear something old and worn, a hoodie if possible. In a rush, he rang off before Emma had a chance to ask or say anything. *Simon was alive! She was going to see Simon.* Wasn't this an illusion? Her heart had suffered so lately, how much more could it take should this not be real? She didn't quite know which way to turn. Nothing seemed real; her knees felt weak, but she must hold up. Think! There wasn't much time to get her wits about her, and she had to dress. After a quick shower and teeth brushing, she pulled on jeans, a hoodie, and hiking shoes—an outfit that she had worn many times to hike with Simon. She then applied a touch of makeup, difficult to do with her hand shaking so, but she needed color not to look so drawn and tired if possible; these past few weeks, drawn and tired had been her permanent self. She felt better than she had thought possible. If this were not real, she didn't know whether she would survive. She brushed her long hair and coiled it up in back, Simon would love to see it, she thought. Simon! He was actually there somewhere; she hadn't imagined it. And calling Major to come with her, she went down.

"Brooks, I haven't time to eat. I'm expecting a helicopter."

"A helicopter, milady?"

"Yes. I can tell you, but please do not mention it to anyone else yet, for I'm not certain it's real . . . but they say Simon is alive, and I'm to be taken to him!" She noticed with curiosity, and wondered why, that Brooks registered little surprise, though he seemed quite happy.

"Alive! What extraordinary news, milady!" Brooks tried to emphasize shock, but in truth, he was but surprised by half. "Ah. Of course," he sought for exactly what to say. "And I'll wrap up something for you to eat on the way. As well, tea to take. I'll bring it to you. Please go on out . . . I hear a helicopter now." And he rushed away to the kitchen before she had time to say, thank you kindly, but she could not possibly eat.

Yes indeed, a roar was coming over. Emma had been rigid with grief, and now she was rigid with anxiety. She felt smothered with the struggle to break through to this new condition. What a cruel joke this had played on so many. She watched the helicopter circle the opening in front of the manor, then settle down. After the blades had slowed their eager pulsing, Agent Collins step down to come for her, just as Brooks raced down the terrace steps with a muffin and a mug of hot tea. Perhaps, in her complete joy and excitement, she could not eat, still he couldn't let her go off without some kind of breakfast.

Collins was pleased to see that she wore jeans and a hoodie, and, unless one really examined her, she bore no immediate resemblance to Lady Haversham. He took her arm and helped her into the machine. She settled in and Brooks handed in the food. She accepted it without knowing what she was doing.

On the way over the land to London, and to the rooftop helipad of MI-5 Command, Emma nervously sipped the tea. It had a calming effect. She held the muffin, still unwrapped, in a tight grip; she didn't think she could move it passed the lump in her throat. As the helicopter settled down on the rooftop, several agents stood aside to welcome Emma and help her step down from the machine. She still held onto the mug of tea and muffin as though they were somehow lifesavers; all she had in the world. Her worried stare took in the agents, who were smiling at her as though she were to be crowned something. Agent Collins gently uncoiled her fingers from around the tea and muffin and deposited them in a nearby bin. Then he led her away from the still-spinning blade. He wanted to hurry lest hostile eyes were taking notice, but it was best to move casually.

"Lady Haversham, welcome to MI-5. We have a surprise for you as promised," he said.

Emma couldn't reply. Her shock that Simon might be in this building, very much alive, seemed to be greater than the shock when she learned that he had been killed. Her mind wanted to rush through memories. She recalled friends who feared for a loved one who had been thought lost on Mount Everest in a storm, and who had incredibly survived the night, and with all ropes gone, found his way down in the dark. The disbelief when he came dragging his near-frozen body into camp had to be the same such as she felt now. After what seemed to be endless walking down stairs and through hallways, she and Agent Collins finally arrived at a door. He knocked. Emma's knees went weak, she nearly dropped, but Collins held her arm and supported her. He fitted his key into the lock, opened the door, and stood back. Emma fell into Simon's arms before she was even certain it was he.

Without a word, Agent Collins shut the door behind them, locked it, and headed down the hall. There was nothing to say or do, nor was there any thought profound enough to express his feelings.

In the room alone, Simon and Emma held each other so tightly they were as one. There were no words. Emma was weak, Simon supported her in his arms, determined never to loosen his grip. She had become so thin there wasn't much to hug—this slight frame. He would be her strength. He thought he had never in his life wanted more than her presence. He drew in deep breaths of her, this woman he had missed so much. In split seconds he reviewed the struggle she had had thinking he was not alive; while he had wanted her, wanted to reassure her, go to her when doing so might have put both of them in danger. In time he would tell her how horrible it had been, his own struggle, but for now, he would not yield his hold on her long enough to find the energy for explanations. There was nothing that could explain—that could convey their feelings.

Emma questioned whether Simon was real. She held on to him, letting him support her. His aroma, that wonderful essence that was Simon; that seemed real enough. She had waited so long with no hope at all, and now to turn a corner and believe this was Simon. For ages it seemed, they stayed tightly embraced.

When their spirits, their acceptance, had calmed a bit, Simon pulled back, looked long at her, then bestowed frantic kisses over her face. Then he release her to stand back again to look at the woman he needed, had yearned for.

"Darling . . . living without you has been the worst ordeal of my life . . . and knowing the grief and sadness you have been living with. I'm so sorry. I love you so much; I wish I could undo it all. It's been my work in Parliament that brought this on us . . . . I thought I was doing something for my country, and I brought destruction on us. Can you ever forgive me?"

She could at last realize that he was real. "Simon, darling, let's not talk about anything except that we are together. I can't believe I'm looking at you. For weeks, I have carried your face in my heart, and now I see it in my eyes as well as in my heart. Please believe that you are a hero, and say no more except how much you love me. You did what a courageous man in service to his country had to do."

Arms tightly enclosed, they felt they would never let go. Nor did they lose touch for the rest of the morning. A few hours later, there was a knock at the door. Simon looked at Emma and said, "Darling, life continues to beckon. It's likely our lunch. Let's eat; we need energy to go on. "Enter," he called out. And Agent Collins entered pushing a trolley covered with the best treats in London.

"Good afternoon, ladies and gentlemen. I'm to advise you that this French restaurant provides only the best," Agent Collins said. "I trust you two, despite your shock, can eat. I had to beat down the chef with one of his very own rolling pins, in order to commandeer the trolley to personally bring you this unexcelled repast. I told our cooks we were entertaining the Queen! And you will see that they . . . bowing to my presumed but misleading authority . . . believed me. And since I understand that royal personages have a healthy appetite, you must not make a liar out of me, though a liar I be."

"Agent Collins," Emma said, "you have been such a friend, such a support, and, you continue to be so." She still had the memory of Simon's arms, felt the assurance that he was real. She could actually welcome this day; the first day she had wanted to welcome in longer than she could imagine. Her heart could open a bit.

Agent Collins had not before seen Emma smile so openly as she did now. "Milady, I trust you will find something tempting on this tray. And in celebration, the chef has included a bottle of Champagne." As he set about moving the savory dishes from the cart to a table over by the window, he acted as though this were an everyday occurrence. "I apologize but the drapery must be kept closed." Could they ever be normal, he wondered; their shock appeared to have them in chains. "Come now," he urged. "Don't let these dishes grow cold. Else I must have them carried over to the Queen, and the Queen does not like leftovers." He looked with compassion at Simon and Emma. Agent Collins' kind face had not grown cynical or testy within the secretive, sometimes vile, work he had had to perform over the years.

"Come dear," Simon urged. "I've grown to know that Agent Collins is not to be crossed. I'm certain that he measures how much we will eat, and it had better be a certain amount or we'll be in trouble. We do not want to incur that risk; I have no doubt that he marks it on a chart just outside the door." He could poke fun now. "And you've grown so thin, my love. I'm going to have to measure what *you* eat, if you don't take care."

Emma managed a slight laugh. Though she knew these two men to be capable of much humor, it seemed to be the first humor on which she could concentrate. Simon felt the warmth of her laugh, its reassurance that they were going to continue. Both wondered whether they could sit apart long enough to feel normal and to eat. "Thank you, Grant," Simon continued, "This is indeed a wonderful feast. I'm positive you have held threats over the chef. Please take him our compliments."

Simon held out Emma's chair and after she was seated, he took the napkin that Agent Collins had arranged beside the plate, and spread it across her lap. "I'm not babying you, Emma, I know you won't allow it for long." She looked up at him with that look, the look she had for only him. "But just allow me to wait on you for today," he said, "and many thousand days following. You are my tonic, and I have been ill for lack of it. I needn't be ashamed before Agent Collins to show my devotion to you. If he's heard nothing at all for the past weeks, he knows about my devotion to Lady Emma Haversham . . . my dear, dear wife." He gently touched her hair that had fallen and had become tousled; he seemed to love her most when she was slightly tousled.

After he opened the champagne and filled their glasses, Agent Collins said, "I must leave now. I'll return later for the trolley."

"Grant, you would make a marvelous waiter," Simon said. "Should you ever need a recommendation, just ask us."

"Thank you, sir. I can't think of a better recommendation, and if you two don't remain safe I may need just that." His eyes levelled Simon with meaning. "It's comforting to know that I have a potential occupation waiting in the sidelines; perhaps even more rewarding than the present one." Then Collins put on his serious face to say, "Brace yourselves, for there's to be a meeting this evening about how best to proceed with you. Exactly what to do next. Whatever it will be, it must be done swiftly."

He left, locking the door behind him. Though there were important issues to discuss with them, right now, they needed to be alone. Moreover, at this time, he didn't want to burden them with more reality. Until Command was able to take the remaining terrorist, and quickly before he organized new threats, Lord Haversham was still in danger. And also, possibly Lady Haversham.

A bit more relaxed and appetites having somewhat returned, Emma and Simon ate—though it wasn't so easy to eat with one hand, as they held on to each other. "How can I ever let go of you again?" Simon asked. "Do you think we can manage to ride Bud and Maggie while we hold hands? If not, I shall never ride again." His teasing was back. That soft lovely teasing Emma enjoyed.

"How you do go on," she said, holding back a tear. And in between savoring the marvelous lunch, her smile washed over Simon like a warm breeze on a cold day. *The quality of mercy falls on all below.*

Simon wanted to catch up on news from Cav Neumont, wanted to ask her all the questions that had been waiting in his mind, but not yet, not while he could think of nothing but gazing at her. Agent Collins had supplied him with the briefest of briefs, but he wanted to hear all of it from Emma's lips. "It would be fatuous of me to ask how you have been," he said. "I can imagine; can know in my heart that you've been far worse than I have, for I *knew* you were alive, and that we would be together again. So many times I've remembered that silly young woman I pulled out of a hedge that day. You wouldn't even speak to me, and I could hardly speak to you. We both thought the other to be intensely arrogant. And yet the Universe arranged for us to fall in love, arranged for us to marry. And, Emma, I've been so happy having you in my life. Peter has been happy having you for step-mother. And you created New Chance which has brought so many people together. Even my stuffy neighbors would miss you, should you disappear from our lives."

"Simon, you must stop. Don't say anything except how much you love me. I have been sick, as you must know, and now, I think I can become well. I can put aside the many days I woke thinking this day will be my last."

Though the plates of food looked exquisite, within their excitement they could eat but little, and when they could eat no more, they sat on the couch and talked about the future. Simon wanted to know how Peter went on, and how the others went on: Lady Mardling, Lady Southway, John Britely, Hannah, the staff. What all had they been about? He wanted to know all that Emma could think of. He hadn't been able to call anyone, and he imagined how surprised they would be when it was thought safe to acknowledge that he was alive and well. In particular he grieved that he hadn't been able to contact Peter, and he hoped that this afternoon Command would give the okay for himself to return home tomorrow. He had worried about Peter. Beginning from when the lad was two-years-old he had raised him as his own son.

"Peter is as well as can be expected," Emma said. "He has taken most of the summer off to help us. We have helped each other."

With Simon's arm around her, she leaned into him; they held hands so tightly she thought they might weld together. She couldn't imagine the moment when again they had to be apart.

In the evening, Agent Collins arrived with his boss, Special Agent Wayfield. Meetings had been held about the best way to proceed regarding Simon's safety, and with but one terrorist yet to be taken it was decided fairly safe to allow Simon to leave Thames House. Perhaps it was pointless to keep him any longer from his family. After greetings were exchanged and coffee was served, Special Agent Wayfield said, "We're most sorry, Sir Simon and Lady Haversham, to have put you through the subterfuge and the ordeal of the past weeks. And were it within our power to have made it easier for either of you we would gladly have done so. And now the consensus is that you may go home. However, we recommend that you install at the manor a specialist in security. Also, this person should take a look at any possible security he can install for New Chance . . . for our sake, as well as for yours." Simon squeezed Emma's hand as if it were his lifeline. "Gather what you need to take with you," Agent Wayfield continued, "and be ready for the chopper tomorrow early. Before dawn. I'll have someone drive down your bags."

15

Brooks watched the helicopter circle the manor, then tilt toward the front loop. Hearing the whop-whop-whop, he had stepped out and craned his neck to see this unusual event. It had happened but once before when Lady Emma had been taken off somewhere, he knew not where, and he thought it had something to do with MI-5's continuing search for those who had killed Lord Haversham. *Killed him?*" Brooks had indications to the contrary about which he kept silent. Now the helicopter settled down not far from the mansion's entrance, but the engine had not stopped and the rotor blades were turning. Brooks kept his distance and waited. He thought he saw four people onboard. Two, he thought were pilots. Two, he knew were passengers, and one was—he was certain—Lady Emma. The fourth? Something familiar about the fourth sitting in the shadow.

Now the blades had slowed, the side panel opened and one of the pilots descended. He turned and reached up a hand—Brooks could see—for Lady Emma. Brooks waited; too soon to venture forth to welcome her, blades turning still. Now he rushed forward with a yell—a yell that not since playing cowboys and Indians, American style, age six, had escaped his lips, and certainly not since he had begun his employment with Lord Haversham—for descending from the helicopter, if he could believe it, was

Lord Haversham—in the flesh, thinner, but wearing a smile. Brooks rushed to him and whooped again, almost in Simon's ear, as he threw his arms around his employer; an unprecedented move. He couldn't help it, had reacted spontaneously, his cells taking over, unable to restrain themselves.

Simon returned the embrace; he knew how his devoted butler had grieved right along with family and friends.

Brooks quickly pulled back. "I'm so sorry your lordship, I was overcome."

"I understand, Brooks. I am as well. It's a time for overcoming. It's wonderful to see you and to be home again. Though I knew that you had everything under the best of care, I have worried so about everyone: you, the manor, and the entire staff."

Within minutes word spread throughout all the staff, upstairs and downstairs. Happy to have his lordship back, all work ceased while they swapped expressions of incredulous wonder and tried to wrap their hearts around belief.

But perhaps the person happiest of all the staff was John Britely. Having no idea of any possibility of Simon's existence, he had silently wept, alone, away from his loving partner, Hannah. Wept until no molecule of moisture descended from his red tired eyes. But knowing the manor's demands, he had continued to turn his thoughts and hands to the work. It would be wrong to say that he had gotten over, accepted the tragedy, but he had pushed all that down, the manor had to be maintained, and with Emma's and Peter's and Hannah's help, the work could continue as Simon wished.

Alone at work in the study over the manor's books, John had not heard the commotion, the faint sound of the helicopter had not entered his consciousness, and when he heard familiar steps, he looked up to see Lady Joan. So strange, that ghost's presence since the disaster; so strange her perpetual smile, not like her in the old days. *Her* steps were silent, and yet the sound of steps continued—familiar. Taking a scant glance to the side, he saw a reflection in a mirror. Following that, he took a determined look toward the door, and saw Simon advance. Simon! *Simon had become a ghost!*

Wearing a smile of understanding, Simon advanced a step into the room. John felt fear, needed to wake up, needed to pinch himself; shivers waved through his body as he stood motionless, paused over the books. Whatever he had done, he didn't deserve the punishing unreality of thinking Simon was back, when he knew it was impossible.

"Relax, my good friend," Simon said. He thought John might pass out. "You're not losing your senses . . . I'm real."

John was unable to move. Simon waited. John looked down at the figures before him. Surely, when he looked again, Simon's image would be gone. But it was not.

"Simon?" he said tentatively.

"Yes, John."

"Is it really you?"

Simon continued to stand in place. "Yes, John. You must believe me. I'm so sorry for playing with your senses and feelings, but it was imperative. MI-5 decreed the fact of my survival to be kept secret." He took another step into the room and spread his arms, but John did not move. Simon waited. Then, slowly, they moved toward each other.

When John was four steps from Simon, he reached out his hand—way out—as though it might be dangerous to do so. Simon, seeing the fear in John's eyes, and the tremble in his hand, grasped John's hand and held it firmly within both of his own until John felt his warmth.

"Sir," John gasped.

"Yes."

John wanted to say something, anything, something such as, "Welcome back," but he choked. He did not know what had happened; did not know what had taken Simon away, or what had brought him back, or whether he had fallen into a trance, but he would accept it. Gladly.

As they stood shaking hands, wondering whether life could be perfect again, Major bounded into the room anxious to jump all over Simon; to ask him where on earth he had been, and why for so long. "I'm back Major," Simon said, petting the dog and ruffling his hair. "I know, my good pet, that you and John have been taking good care of Lady Haversham."

He was back.

Then the men hugged for the first time—the gravity of relief pulling them together. John's knees near collapse, he had to sit before his legs gave out.

After the news was digested that Lord Haversham had indeed escaped death, and after the staff had grown calm about it, John Britely held a staff meeting. He wanted, not only to bring all together to celebrate, but as well, to assure that they must continue precautions for keeping the manor secure. "We'll be letting a flat in the south courtyard for a security specialist I've employed. He'll be about installing alarms, as well as watching all around the premises for any unusual activity. Please understand that Lord Haversham feels terrible about the deaths of his colleagues," he said to the group. "It might take him time to be his normal self. Don't rush him please. When you encounter him about the course of your day, just be yourself; he will appreciate that. Obviously he couldn't help what happened. And as well, knowing how hard this has been on you, he has been concerned about all of you. He'll be down shortly to talk to you himself." As he spoke, John had to dab at moisture in his eyes, hard to hold back as, indeed, all those around him found to be so.

That evening the staff had been asked to join family and friends in the drawing room to hear Simon's story, though he hadn't much to tell. And Agent Collins had arrived with Schrödinger who had taken possession of a close spot by the earl's foot. Lady Mardling, Lady Southway, and Hannah hadn't yet recovered their tongues for this surprise, and without a word they sat to attention. The group was silent as the grave; the staff standing tentatively frozen in wait to hear the earl. He looked at them with concern—and love.

"I was running late leaving Westminster, and when the bomb exploded; I hadn't reached the exit," Simon said. "Sorry to say, two of my colleagues were killed. I should have been leaving with them, but was held back for a phone call. In some sense, my beloved wife saved me, for it was the call I had requested from the airline letting me know her flight's ETA. You may recall that she was returning from her aunt's funeral in New York. After that, internet chatter said that I was the target, and I was swept into a safe room so fast, I was dizzy. In fact I was locked up . . . locked up all this time. After I absorbed that shock, and realized that I wouldn't be released, I still had my mobile and so I phoned Lady Emma to say I was all right, but Agent Collins burst into the room," he smiled in Collin's direction, "and snatched the phone. I felt as a naughty schoolboy must feel. My word, they were determined to keep me isolated and safe; I'm not sure my hide is worth it."

Amidst tears, there was a gentle titter of laugh through the group; he had managed to lighten the room's air.

"I wasn't allowed to contact anyone, nor even let them know I was okay. The man in charge of me, Agent Grant Collins . . . ," He gave a nod to the agent, "said you would be watched as well. New Chance would be watched. I understand that a security expert, a Mr. Tyler Brotherton, has just been hired and will have a flat in the south court. We'll follow his advice."

On hearing this, Corky's heart executed a flip-flop: Tyler a security expert? This must be a mistake; she could only wait and see.

"One of the terrorist is still extant," Simon continued, "but his holdout is known and he'll be taken soon. As he surrounds himself with women and children, authorities have had to delay in snatching him." He paused his speech to look around thoughtfully at every face. "And so, I have hurt you all, but I fear my dear wife," he took Emma's hand, "and Peter, have been hurt the most, for they are the ones I routinely annoy the most."

"Actually, Father, your absence gave us a break," Peter laughed; his eyes warm with emotion.

16

Now that Tyler Brotherton had stopped coming into The Bucket, Corky had no one with whom to flirt. It was quite shocking that he would be living in a courtyard flat at the manor. Even though that flat was not at all near the courtyard with hers and Troy's flat, still their paths might cross. She longed to ask Tyler why he kept away from The Bucket. Was it something she had said? Meanwhile, her patience was called on to deal with Troy. He was a changed man; more boring than ever, always touting his knowledge about the museum-quality pieces in the manor; reminding Corky how he could, without referring to his notes, answer any question the public asked, and then some. He had gone beyond the requirement—that to become the docent he had to know the artifacts in the rooms open to the public—to spouting the manor's history when he had an audience. Patiently he would wait for Corky to come in from work; patiently would wait while she freshened up, changed into something fetching. His brain would be full of something new, perhaps about the book in Queen Ann's portrait. The book's importance would have ruled Troy's day, and he wanted eagerly for Corky to appreciate it as well. At first Corky listened with feigned interest. Uh huh. Uh huh, she would say while examining her fingernails and calculating how soon she could get out the door. Now she found his lectures to be heavy, too heavy to absorb, especially after a day's work. Aside from being happy with her job in the manor's kitchen, she didn't care a Tupp-be-damned about the manor's artifacts, and was tired of hearing Troy go on about them. So at the end of her workday, while listening for a decent interval to Troy, as usual she borrowed the golf cart and drove down to The Bucket.

Sometimes, before he left for Craig-on-Wold and home, Edward Fitzpatrick would sit in The Bucket's back booth for dinner, and whereas before he saw that Corky had company when she sat at the bar, lately she was always alone. Tonight he decided to sit at the bar. Perhaps he could chat her up. He understood, indeed had overheard, that she worked at the manor, and that information had stirred for him an idea. He took a seat, said hello to Barney, the bartender, and waited. Soon Corky came in.

"How're you keeping, Corky?" Barney asked, when she had taken a seat at the bar.

"Same, Barney. As irritable tonight as a dog with fleas."

"Indeed. What's the problem?"

"Troy. Now that he's the docent for the manor, he thinks he's Picasso, or one of those chaps. He thinks the manor is the Tate. Isn't that a museum in London?"

"I think it might be."

Barney poured the usual for Corky, and turned to Edward who had signaled for a refill. Edward took his glass and moved down next to Corky.

"I'm Edward Fitzpatrick. I believe I've seen you in here before." He looked her over with eyes of appreciation.

Slightly taken back, but only for three seconds, she sized up this new opportunity and found it appealing. "Name's Corky. Pleased to meet you." She fingered the front of her dress as though she might not be put together just right. "I've just come in from work and didn't take time to change," she said, ignoring the fact that for nearly twenty minutes she had swapped out frocks trying to decide which one suited her most.

"I see . . . not to worry. You would be pretty in anything; some women are like that . . . ." He thought he might have good reason to pour it on. "But few." He let a few seconds elapse for her to take in his flattery. "And do you live in the village?" he asked.

"I live with me mate in a flat at the manor house . . . where I work." She was proud to say this.

"What's it like working at the manor?" He would not say that he had had dinner there when Lady Southway—Charlotte—had invited him. Wouldn't let on that he knew Lady Southway.

"It's okay. I work in the kitchen, and we have plenty good food working there, a real benefit. And the kitchen manager, Mrs. Ogilvy is easy enough. We get along fine."

"What complaint do you have then? I think I heard you complain to Barney about something."

"Oh not about my job. It's about me mate, Troy. He's pumped up with himself ever since they made him docent. Has a swell head now. Taken to learn'n even. Can't stop gushing facts: facts, facts, facts. I have to get out of the flat!"

"And that's why you come here for your evening meal?"

"Exactly." She held his eyes for as long as she dared.

Out of the side of his eyes, Barney watched. Every night up to recent days, he had noticed that Corky always had a man's attention. However, this was a different man, the one who prefers the back corner. He thought these men didn't live in the village, for by now Barney knew nearly every village resident. He had wondered about the strangers coming in every night lately. It wasn't his business, but he knew Corky, and had wondered what was up with her and Troy. They used to come in together.

Corky seemed quite pleased to have Edward's attention; indeed, flattered. She had become more popular than she was used to, and she intended to keep up a lively conversation with Mr. Fitzpatrick.

"What a good thing it is that you're happy with your employment," Edward said. "And what hours do you work? I've always heard that manor staff are terribly overworked and dispatched to dank cellar rooms."

"Not at Cav Neumont Manor. When the earl modernized, he had the kitchen and pantries moved up to the ground floor. We even have windows. There are several of us cooks and we work different hours. I open up most days and help with cooking breakfast. Then I clean up and begin chopping stuff for lunch and dinner, and sometimes I make a sauce. That leaves my evenings free so I can come in here. I used to chat here with a gentleman, but he don't come in anymore." She gave Edward a big smile, to show how liberated she was.

"You open up?" He paused while Corky's head bobbed up and down. "So you must have your own key. I heard somewhere that the manor had to be kept locked up tight ever since that awful business about the earl."

"Right. I have the key to the kitchen entrance, and the last cook out at night locks up. We must do our part to help with security. These days, we're all concerned about security." She formed a smug mouth and gave her most important up-and-down nod for emphasis. "Lives may be at stake."

"Then you have a position of considerable trust."

"Right. You know, Mrs. Ogilvy and other staff live there . . . three floors up. I live in a courtyard flat and most mornings get to the kitchen before they're down."

It had become important now for Edward Fitzpatrick to talk to Corky; important to gain her friendship and trust. And many evenings he looked into the tavern, driving over from Craig-on-Wold. She was always there, and he sensed that she looked for him. He bought her drinks, and as well on some nights, her dinner. He would sit in the back booth and order for her. Then, as she was leaving, he would hold her jacket. Not used to such genteel thoughtfulness, she found herself nearly quivering as would a scared kitty. Troy was completely unaware of these little courtesies, and Corky keenly felt the difference. During the day, her thoughts were on Edward, and getting herself to The Bucket, hoping he would be there. He had said that he volunteered at New Chance one day a week, and lived in Craig-on-Wold, a considerable drive, and yet he managed to meet her at The Bucket more evenings than not. Corky wondered why.

Edward wondered whether anyone would take an interest in his spending so much time talking to Corky, but as he looked about, he saw no interest and no familiar faces. He wondered whether he should ask her not to mention meeting him, but decided that the kitchen gossip would stay in the kitchen. As well, he was wary of putting Corky on guard, wary of causing her suspicion. He continued to volunteer at New Chance, and continued to keep Lady Charlotte Southway in thrall. She had had a bleak existence in the village, living alone, with only Lady Mardling and the Havershams for occasional company. It had been an easy thing for Edward to work his way into New Chance and into Charlotte's acquaintance. He had been supplied with a story about his father's death, and supplied with numerous artifacts, used clothing, and bric-a-brac to bring as donations; grow the volunteers' complete faith in him. Who would suspect someone who came in with so many valuable donations to have an ulterior motive?

However, Edward decided nothing was to be learned at New Chance. No one at the shop, including

Charlotte, mentioned Lord Haversham's name, or even that the earl might still be alive. It was as though their lips were sealed regarding the earl. When Edward would ask Lady Charlotte about the earl, she would always reply that she was really out of touch. And so Edward hoped instead to find a way for his connection to Corky to pay off.

For a while the situation at the manor and in the village went on in this manner: slowly the excitement of Lord Haversham's return calmed, and the work of the manor proceeded. Good meals were abundant—the table groaned with the dishes Mrs. Ogilvy and staff prepared. It was as though they felt the need to dress up servings more than ever, hoping that would show Lord Haversham their pleasure that he was with them. And good company would drop in, as though the presence of each and every one would further guarantee his lordship's security. This included Lady Mardling, Lady Southway, and sometimes Mars and Sophia, from Wickenbird Farm. These were all good friends who loved and amused each other.

Though, in her heart, Corky knew not to mention that his lordship had returned to the manor unscathed, the importance to be gained by telling about it was too significant to withhold, and she told Edward and Barney all about it. Edward managed to feign that, though he was glad the earl was okay, he had no particular interest in the matter. Actually, the fact of Lord Haversham's being alive and well, had not been a total shock to Edward; he had inside information. He was told about the cat that appeared now at the manor, and now at Thames House, he had been told about the helicopter. There was sufficient evidence that his lordship was very much alive. It was Edward's job to help do something about that. Until he figured out what action that should be, and how it should be attempted, he would continue his connection to Lady Charlotte Southway (the comrades had praised him for working his way into

New Chance), as well as continue to promote his association with Corky. He needed all the sources of information about Lord Haversham he could gather. He couldn't see how this might turn out, but it might prove profitable.

At the manor, there was much discussion about Edward; the idea that a gentleman was enthusiastic about volunteering at a thrift shop. Some said he needed to find fulfilment by helping. Some asked whether he couldn't have found it in Craig-on-Wold near where he lived, rather than make the drive to Cav Neumont Village. On the occasion back before the earl had returned home, when Edward had accompanied Lady Southway to the manor for dinner, Lord Haversham's name had not been mentioned and the invitation had not been repeated.

On that occasion, taking her arm, John Britely had managed to pull Charlotte aside as the party was going through to dinner. "Lady Southway, please forgive me for asking, but you must understand our position. What does Mr. Fitzpatrick do that he can spare his time to volunteer at New Chance? We can't be too careful, you know." With the requirement for security, and the knowledge that this surprising new volunteer seemed to be hanging in, John had felt constrained to asked questions he would not otherwise have asked.

"Of course, John, I completely understand. We must all be careful. Edward is a science journalist. He writes for publications such as *Science Bulletin Monthly*. I believe he is a physicist, though he has not said directly. On the days he's not at New Chance, he is usually at Oxford or Cambridge attending seminars, or interviewing his connections. And he writes at his home in Craig-on-Wold. He's a neighbor of Lady Claire's friend there, a Mr. Oliver somebody; I haven't heard his last name." She nodded her head with assurance. "He's been quite kind to me, but like anyone else, we can be fooled." Saying this, Charlotte felt sad. She wished she knew Edward better; knew more about him. You would think that once in a while he would discuss something on which he was working, an article he had published, or perhaps a Nobelist he had interviewed. But Edward's life was sharply compartmented: he spoke only of events at New Chance, or events in Craig-on-Wold. Once Charlotte had asked him what physics or cosmology study he was undertaking at that time, and he said only that it was top secret.

"The world of physics and cosmology is highly competitive," he had said, "and scientists must keep their research a secret until ready to publish their findings. If they don't, others will . . . and sometimes quite easily . . . steal their ideas for their own." And Edward had no more to tell Lady Southway about his work.

She had to be content with that, hadn't asked again. On the days she worked at New Chance, she rose earlier than usual, took more care of her appearance, put on lipstick, and tweaked her cheeks. Then, she brushed her hair out into a golden fluff. She applied a couple drops of scent, and as she did so, she listened to her heart; it was full of Edward. He had given special attention to no one but her. And when he singled her out, had he understood that she was the only unattached woman working for New Chance? Obviously Emma's heart was taken. Lady Mardling's life was entwined with Count Bianco who increasingly came out from London to spend time with her. Hannah and John's closeness was wedge-proof. Sophia had moved from Firefly Cottage on Lord Haversham's estate to Wickenbird Farm and had married Mars Marsden. Only Lady Southway's heart went unclaimed. Therefore, when Edward showed up and began hanging around New Chance—getting to know everyone—Lady Southway marveled that he had shown a particular interest in herself; came in only when she was working. And as she had chosen to stay in Cav Neumont Village, and stay in the lovely villa her late husband had left to her, she had never had expectations for another man in her life: one just for her.

Now, on a few evenings when Edward wasn't looking for Corky, he asked Lady Southway to dinner at The Meridian. This did not occur frequently enough for Charlotte, quite hopeful for more. However it went, though slowly, Lady Southway had to accept it; she was not one to be the aggressor.

But, when one day Lady Mardling said that Edward had been in The Bucket the night before, sitting at the bar with a woman—flirting, Lady Southway had to think. Had he said he would be staying over at The Meridian that night? Well, it didn't matter; he had not declared himself to her in the slightest, he was a free man. Although, recalling his manner toward her, she knew that he had been showing particular fondness for her. Leading her on, some would say, and she wanted to follow. Charlotte did not let on that Lady Mardling's information hurt. Still, she did want to ask Edward about this. Indirectly.

The next day that the two of them were together at New Chance, during a lull, Lady Southway worked up her courage to so discretely find out something about this; that Edward would not suspect her intentions.

"Oh, Edward, the other night at The Bucket, did you meet Lady Mardling's gentleman friend, Count Bianco? He and Aggie are quite close, you know. She said she saw you there." Did this sound like probing? She hoped not; she wasn't good at this.

Woops. Well, Edward knew it would happen. He knew enough people in Cav Neumont now, that he was bound to be seen by one of them when he didn't intend to be. He knew this, and yet he also knew that it was potentially important to keep things moving forward with Corky. Both she and Lady Southway were important to him for different reasons.

"Ah, yes. Indeed I was there. However, I did not see Lady Mardling." He wondered when she had seen him. He supposed he was seated with his back to her as he sat at the bar talking, flirting—truth be told—with Corky; he hoped not too obviously. "At the inn as I worked, I had stressed out so with the documents I was trying to understand, that I temporarily gave up and went to relax at The Bucket with a glass of ale." Attempting to be as natural as possible, he set to work folding jeans onto a shelf. "I had planned only to have a glass at the bar and head back to the inn and continue working, but straightway a woman took the stool next to me, and she would not stop talking and asking me questions. I found myself having to be polite. She was a nuisance." He thought that Lady Southway happily accepted this. Though the situation and timing were all wrong, Charlotte had become important to him. He wanted to see more of her but circumstances would not allow. He must persevere down the path he had begun with Corky. Sadly, he thought, he had a mission, a conflicting one, conflicting with his heart. Life could be quirky that way: throwing something you wanted right at your feet while showing you that you must reject it.

17

W here is Edward today?" Lady Claire asked Lady Southway. Claire had come in with her arms full of large colorful paper umbrellas ready to change the window display.

"In Oxford. He said he had to attend an important seminar and it was only for today."

"Oxford? Hmm. I wonder why he had to go there. When he popped in for drinks last night he didn't mention it to Oliver and me."

"He's quite modest about his knowledge, his contacts. Never talks about his work."

"His work?" Claire exclaimed.

"Right. Sometimes he mentions an article he's writing."

"He writes articles!"

"Yes. I'm surprised you and Oliver haven't heard about that."

Claire didn't reply; she had to think about this. She and Oliver had entertained Edward a few times. He lived alone and, as a friendly neighbor in the village of Craig-on-Wold where Claire spent many nights, inviting him over for dinner was a natural thing to do. But she had understood that Edward was unemployed and living on an inheritance. He did go to London on occasion, but he had not ever mentioned anything about going elsewhere. And they had just seem him last night; he had said nothing about attending a seminar in Oxford. She wanted to know more about this.

"Are you certain, Charlotte?" Claire asked.

"Why, yes. He's a science writer for two, I think it is, journals. And for this he must go to Oxford or Cambridge for seminars or interviews. Sometimes he interviews our top physicists. He's quite modest about it, though."

Claire stared at Charlotte. She couldn't imagine that during drinks or dinners with Edward, that he wouldn't have mentioned his career, meanwhile speaking about it all to Charlotte. Charlotte looked so convinced that Claire decided she would not discuss this further until she had a chance in the evening to talk it over with Oliver.

Lady Southway wondered why Edward had not mentioned his science writing to Claire or to Oliver. Although he hadn't discuss it widely, he had been quite specific that he was a science journalist, and was often in Oxford or Cambridge. A charming man, nice to look at and quite attentive, she had found herself drawn to him; she enjoyed working with him at New Chance. She thought about the chance that first brought him into the shop when he came in with donations, and seeing her stress at the time, had offered to help. And, he had taken her to dinner a few times, shown a particular fondness for her—caught and held her glance far longer than necessary. And, on one occasion, she had invited him to come with her to the manor for dinner. Emma had welcomed him. He must be for real.

"Oliver, dear," Lady Claire started, "something strange about Edward. He has told Lady Charlotte Southway that he is a science journalist, and that requires him at times to go to Oxford or Cambridge."

"A journalist? Amazing thought. Could she be mixing him with someone else?"

"No. They have worked together once a week for several weeks or more, and have had a few dinners together. She's getting to know him quite well."

"Why would he tell her that, when as we know he's completely unemployed, lives on an inheritance. At least, that's what he tells us. And I don't think he would have a reason to keep from you and me that he's a science journalist."

"He wasn't at New Chance today. Had told Lady Charlotte beforehand that he had to be in Oxford for a physics seminar. She says that he can't discuss his work due to the competition among physicists."

"Hmm. Perhaps when you have a chance to speak with her privately you could tell her what we know of him. Might he be putting her on? Though I can't imagine why. Why would he not want her to know his income is inherited?"

So it was, that on the next opportunity, Lady Claire asked Lady Southway to step out with her for lunch. "Delighted, Claire." Charlotte said. "You and I never have a chance to talk as in the old days." (The old days were before Lord Haversham had met Emma; the days when Lady Mardling and Lady Southway were, so they thought, in line to become Lord Haversham's next intended.)

The women walked over to The Meridian and took a table near the fireplace. Though the days were hot now, those old stone buildings held on to the cold like an old man holding on to his sweater.

"Let's celebrate. Let's have a martini," Lady Claire said. She wanted courage to discuss this strange business regarding Edward Fitzpatrick, for Claire had seen Charlotte's preference for Edward—and as well, it seemed to be mutual. And undeniably, there were reports that he had been seen at The Bucket flirting with some woman.

After their martinis arrived and they had toasted the fine afternoon, clearing her throat Claire began. "My dear, please forgive my intrusion, but there's something puzzling about Mr. Fitzpatrick."

Lady Southway pulled a question over her face and stared at Lady Claire.

"He has said to you that he is a science journalist."

"Yes. He has. He is indeed."

"You know that he is Oliver's neighbor."

"Right. He drives over from Craig-on-Wold."

"You might know that Oliver and I are close . . . very close, and I am often at Oliver's, and he and I have entertained Edward on several occasions."

"Yes. I believe I did know that," Lady Southway said.

"Well, he has never mentioned to us that he is a science journalist. Don't you think, that if he talks about it to you, that it would be natural for him to talk about it with us? He tells us that he is unemployed and living on an inheritance."

Lady Southway speared a large green stuffed olive from a plate the waiter had placed on their table. After careful thought she said, "He doesn't actually talk about it." Though she had no wish to think suspiciously about Edward, she had had to force down a few questions that had risen lately. "He has mentioned only that that is what he does; why he often goes up to Oxford." She bit into the olive hoping that this would be the end of this topic.

"Look into it, Charlotte," Lady Claire said. "Ask him a few questions about physics, or about the Universe. See how he replies. It's not so much that you should make it your business . . . it's just strange . . . on the whole quite mysterious."

Oops, this topic is not over, Charlotte thought, as she choked down the remainder of the olive. "I have already. He dances around the topic, revealing nothing. I even asked him to show me an article he had published, and he said that they are stored in a vault, together with a copy of the journal."

While she pondered her uncomfortable feeling for blaspheming Edward, she speared another one of those savory olives stuffed with something. "Umm . . . wonderful." And for a moment, while she remembered his excuses, she savored the olive. "But on the other hand, he has explained that he cannot discuss new theories and discoveries, until they're actually published."

Dropping the topic, Claire took a tiny sip of her martini and scanned the menu. She had left enough hints; she wanted to let Charlotte find her own attitude about Edward. The women ordered and tried to enjoy the gourmet dishes, but their thoughts were not on the excellence of the food, but on questions about Edward.

The following week seemed to Lady Charlotte Southway to have no end. Pondering Lady Claire's intrusion, she told herself that Claire could be mischievous. Still, Claire had been dead serious. Unable to rest her mind about the mystery attached to Edward's career, or lack of career, she counted the minutes until she saw him again. She explored various ways to confront him about his work. She would tell herself to forget it, it wasn't her business. And anyway, he and she were not tied together. Then in the next breath his statements to her about his trips and meetings would insist themselves into her thoughts. Even though she knew there was no serious reason that it should matter to her—it did. She had to admit to her secret self a fondness for him that included certain hopes.

The next day that they worked together, she was prepared with a technique to find out something, solve this quandary.

"It's amazing, isn't it," she began, "what the LHC is doing!"

Edward looked at her with a completely blank expression. "The what?" he asked.

"The LHC. You know, the Large Hadron Collider."

His blank expression remained. "The large . . . ?"

"You know . . . the beam splitter; smashes protons, or perhaps it's photons, together. Or, for all I know, maybe it's marbles." She had done a bit of research. In trying to keep it light, as though unconcerned, she accompanied this tricky inquisition with a soft laugh.

"Right." Edward recovered and caught up somewhat. He recalled vaguely hearing something about a collider. "I can't discuss the latest findings, for, as I might have mentioned, competition among physicists is fierce, and until it's in print, I can't discuss information I might be gathering for an article."

True, Charlotte thought; he had said that before. Well, she would accept that for now. But, she wondered about it, and as well, about his questions to her about goings-on at the manor; such as when its residents were in or were out. He appeared to be unduly interested. So on the next occasion that they worked together, she had researched further on the Internet, and was ready with another question about cosmology.

"Edward, did you see the latest news . . . that a group of cosmologists have found that another universe might be bumping up against ours?" Edward looked puzzled as though he hadn't heard this. "And some cosmologists think that might be why our Universe's gravity field is so weak . . . because it's leaking into the other universe." *Listen to me*; she amazed herself sounding so informed.

How to reply to her? If he could help it, he never read an article about gravity, or about what is happening to, or what had happened to, or what will happen to our Universe. Whatever it was, he couldn't do anything about it; thus he could let the question rest. But perhaps he should satisfy Charlotte's curiosity. He grabbed her up and swung her around. "Aren't you the strange one worrying about something weird and unholy that can never be proven. And were I to know something about it, I could probably not discuss it." His expression said, *I'm rather smug about this*.

Lady Southway's curiosity was not quelled: in fact she became more curious, for he did not at all seem to know about important recent science news. She suspected that Edward had not heard about the LHC, which was comparable, at least in the world of physics, to not knowing that it rains in England, or, he was clever with bluffing. For now though, she would let it go.

However, it would not be Charlotte's concern for long, for Edward Fitzpatrick, wary about too many questions from her, did not come into New Chance again, nor did he contact her. He merely posted a note that new demands would take up his days and prevent his helping at New Chance. So sorry.

He had sad regrets about this change, but anyway he despaired of learning, while working at New Chance, further news about the earl; when the earl was at home; when he was not. It was time for him to concentrate on his mission. He must shoot an arrow in a different direction.

18

While she hung dresses that had come in recently, Emma noticed a man sitting at the back table drinking tea and reading a newspaper. It was pleasant to see a man there.

Tyler Brotherton was off studying requirements for security at the manor. Edward had stopped coming to volunteer. (And sadly, Charlotte's morale seemed to be taken down a few notches.) Men, Emma felt, contributed their spice and outlook; she was happy to see this new one. He was rather rumpled in his clothing, his shoes were not polished, and he needed a haircut. As well, he was too thin and looked hungry. Still, with all that, he was quite dignified. He appeared to be alone, whereas usually when a man came into New Chance and sat at the tea table, he would be waiting for his wife or companion. Emma stepped over to help a customer and thought no more about him.

The next day he was back, and he seemed eager for a cupcake and muffin that she had fetched from the bakery next door. Emma wondered about him; what was his story? Everyone who came in had a story, some more diverse and strange than others. She thought his must be strange. Yet still, whatever it was, it was his own business. And, he was welcome.

On many of the next days, the scruffy man would be sitting at the back table reading, always minding his business. He bothered no one, paid no attention to the shoppers, and with his intelligent—though tired—face, he was clearly not potty. Now when Emma stepped into the bakery for buns and muffins, she ordered a few extra. As she did so, she pictured the man; not even certain that he would be in. But he was—and he looked up when she came in with the treats. She carried the bakery box to the back where he sat trying to be absorbed in his paper. As she spread out buns and muffins, he looked up and gave her an almost embarrassed smile. His eyes carried a deep tiredness that Emma felt must have old origins.

"Good morning," she said, eager to help him feel comfortable at New Chance. Then she turned away to wait on a customer; she wanted to leave the man, whatever his story was, in peace. When he began coming in regularly, and staying longer, Emma took a break one day to sit at the table with him and have a cup of tea. She wanted to appear as though this were a normal occurrence while learning whether the man would talk; especially talk about himself. Glancing back and forth between rain pelting the window, and customers milling about, she waited. He continued to read, although, Emma thought, he must have read his paper twice over. She scanned the shop, pretending to survey what went on.

After a while she said, "I brought in hard-boiled eggs today. Boiled them myself this morning. Would you like one? I have them in the refrigerator."

It took him five seconds to absorb what she had asked, the question so strange to him. "Yes. Why yes. Yes indeed." He smiled and looked relieved—she might have been asking him to leave—he had been there so often, and had stayed so long.

"The refrigerator is in the storage room," Emma said as she stood and gestured. "I'll be right back with hard-boiled eggs," *in the plural*, she thought: the man is hungry.

On many days following, Emma came in to work with hard-boiled eggs and placed them in a bowl over ice, amongst the muffins and buns. In fact, even on the days when she could have stayed home, she brought in something—not always eggs. Sometimes it was tuna salad with crackers, and carrot sticks. She would place them about in a casual manner as though it were a regular thing to do for shoppers. She had become comfortable with the man's presence, made certain to have a few minutes to sit and give him attention. He was lonely, she thought.

"I'm Emma Haversham," she said to him on one of the many occasions when she stopped for a cup with him. She reached out her hand, and as she was standing, Mr. Hobby stood.

"My name is Hobby," he said, shaking her out-reached hand. "Horace Hobby." He didn't feel the need to reveal more; after all, the woman, Lady Haversham (he knew who she was), would not want anything to do with him, and that would be the end of it.

But it was not to be the end, though he was not to know that yet.

"Do you live in the village, Mr. Hobby?"

"Ah . . . no. . . . I live in my car," he said as he nodded his head in confirmation. Might as well get it out there, he thought; she probably knows everyone in the village, no use to dissemble.

"I see." As though sleeping in one's car was common among the villagers. Choking down all the questions that rose, she understood instantly that this was his truth.

He wanted to keep the topic off himself, so he was quick to say, "It was tragic to learn about Lord Haversham, and subsequently to hear the good news that he had been spared."

109

His speech was refined Emma noticed; whoever he was, he had an educated, enlightened background.

Before Brooks announced dinner that evening while Emma and Simon were having a cocktail with John and Hannah, Emma mentioned Mr. Hobby, and that she had just learned that he lived in his car. "He said he often sits in church and Reverend Austin lets him use the facilities . . . you know." She rolled her eyes. "He always seems clean; he must use a bath there. He also goes to the library in Craig-on-Wold."

"He comes into the shop when I'm there as well," said Hannah. "Keeps to himself, has tea and a bun . . . and an egg, if you've brought some in . . . and reads. He seems quite nice, doesn't bother anyone."

"His name is Hobby, Horace Hobby. And he appears to be down-and-out. If he is, I wish we could help him in some way. More than just giving him a bun."

Through all this, Simon was quiet. His furrowed brow revealed thoughts that, while he struggled to prioritize them, wanted to burst out. "Hobby? He said his name was Hobby?"

"Yes," Emma said. "Horace Hobby."

Simon, with a puzzled look, continued to think for a moment, then said. "He must be that barrister whose case was in the news every day. Do you remember that case, John? It made the daily news."

While John thought about this, the others waited to hear more. "The barrister who was sued for damages, and lost the case?"

"Right. Rumors were that his solicitor fed him incorrect facts about whether a German ship that went down in the Mediterranean had carried insurance," Simon said. "It bankrupted the man, for the prosecutor sued him for everything. And his wife . . . I recall her name was Alice . . . used to the good life, divorced him. Sad case, for in my opinion none of the evidence was persuasive." Simon sipped from his sherry while he recalled the case. "It was well over a year ago. I clearly remember being disappointed with the outcome. Mr. Hobby had a stellar background, but rumors were that his solicitor received kickbacks from a silent investor in Germany. It was never proven."

"Right. I do recall," John said. "And he's now our man at New Chance?" He looked to Emma for confirmation. "He must have had some savings left and when that ran out, he began sleeping in his car. No one could have afforded to hire him."

"Perhaps we can do something for him," Emma said.

Brooks announced dinner and they went through.

While Simon treated Schrödinger with bits from his plate, John described plans for a new plumbing situation at the manor; there was always something. For the time, the topic of Mr. Hobby seemed to be forgotten. Not by Emma though—while the men discussed what to do about plumbing, Emma continued to think about Mr. Hobby and to wonder what he did on Sunday when New Chance was closed. After dinner, when they were back in the library for coffee, she renewed the subject.

"We have that nice little back room with that lovely lie-back leather chair. What if we offer it to Mr. Hobby for a place to sleep so he can be in out of the damp? And with the refrigerator nearby, he can have food. And there's a hot plate that heats our tea water . . . he can heat soup. We can say that he will be doing us a service, acting as watchman." Emma waited. She expected at least one of the group, if not all of them as they sat, mouths open, staring at her, to howl at this surprising suggestion. But there wasn't one peep.

Simon looked quite considered as he said, "He would have to have a key."

His look surprised Emma; he was thinking over her question; not rejecting it out of hand. "Isn't he quite

111

honest?" she asked. "Just had a really bad stroke of luck, something he couldn't control?" Her hope reached out to Simon.

"Let's think about this," Simon said. "Perhaps I should come meet him. Let's talk about this again later."

However, for Emma, there was no 'later.' She abhorred waiting for an outcome when she was certain what the outcome was to be, and the next day, when as usual Mr. Hobby was there for tea, she sat down and very quietly asked, "Mr. Hobby, would you like to sleep in our back room? There's a comfortable reclining lounge chair there. We need a night-watchman." This was a stretch, she laughed to herself, for the only chore to which a night-watchman might apply himself in this quiet village would be to count fireflies, or crickets.

Mr. Hobby's face became a mix of hopelessness and hope, as well as surprise. Before he could answer, Emma said, "Come see."

Mr. Hobby appeared powerless to rise from the chair, as though this might only be a movie unfolding before him. And he looked at her without moving.

"Mr. Hobby allow me to show you what I mean."

He laid down the paper, rose slowly, and hesitantly followed Emma to the back room where, having appeared magically overnight, was a pile of blankets.

"While you are here, you can be our watchman. You can do us a service." Her tone conveyed conviction that Mr. Hobby's sleeping there was a done deal.

Before he could think of what to reply, he had first to overcome the grip in his throat. Emma waited while he commandeered his tongue. "I confess," he said finally, "this is supremely more comfortable than my car. Please allow me to do whatever I can to repay you."

"All I ask, Mr. Hobby, is to allow us the use of the room, if we need it during business hours. Sometimes a customer ducks in here to try on something, and as you can see, we use it for storage that we might need during the day; perhaps a little inconvenient for you at times, but warm and dry. And, Mr. Hobby, the refrigerator is right there," she gestured to a white box standing near a closet door. "We must keep its contents moving so they don't become too old." She said this in an off-hand way as if every storage room was bound to have a refrigerator. "And there's that," she gestured to the hotplate. She picked up her purse and rummaged around in it coming up with a key, which she handed to him. "You must have a key, Mr. Hobby." She began to rush, aware that, above all, she wouldn't allow him to think this offer was charity. She didn't know whether she was more embarrassed than he; it was a sensitive situation.

He accepted the key as though it might burn his hand. He hardly knew what he was doing. Then he turned around to look at the lounge chair with longing. *The gentle rain*, he thought.

Emma felt the embarrassment that Mr. Hobby felt, and she turned to the door. "I must see whether a customer needs help." And with a rather warm feeling—it was not often that one could do something that brought such an emotional reward—Emma quickly left the room to wait on a customer.

Mr. Hobby closed the back storeroom door, and without a nod to anyone left the store. Even though it was gently raining, overcome with Emma's generosity, he had to get out and walk, or sit on a bench in the green while he pulled in his emotions. So often rainy weather had challenged his resources, and now he would gladly accept the mercy of New Chance's warmth: this night he would not have to sleep in his damp car. This would be such a blessing he could, just thinking ahead, already feel the dry warmth of the New Chance back room. He could actually read at night whilst keeping warm and dry.

Mr. Hobby, always tidy, leaving no trace of domestication in the back room, turned out to be fully welcome to sleep at the shop. Emma, Lady Mardling, Lady Southway, and Hannah, taking a tea break at times, would chat with him when he was in. They were growing fond of him. Emma, in particular began to want a more regular life for him than that of sleeping in the back room. The thought kept occurring to her that with so many rooms at the manor why couldn't he have a room there to himself. And that thought wouldn't leave her alone. Finally one evening when she and Simon were catching up on the daily news, she broached the subject.

"What if we offer Mr. Hobby a room here?" She looked at Simon with a look that said, *you know there's no good reason not to.* She waited for Simon's response. "He's so proud that we would have to couch the offer in terms of his helping us somehow," Emma said, before Simon could get his thoughts together. "I've given the idea much consideration, and since we're told to be hyper-secure here, doors locked all the time, be on guard constantly . . . and Mr. Brotherton is merely to establish alarms and such . . . perhaps we could tell Mr. Hobby that we need an internal watchman; another set of eyes and ears, someone in the building. And you know there's a room down the hall from the kitchen . . . we can say we need a watchman on the ground floor, near the rear. I doubt he would be contented with that forever, his mind is so vastly trained, but it might help him to reconstruct his legal practice . . . to have a private warm and dry place of his own . . . you know, a proper desk and so on."

Yet Simon had not replied—too many ideas coming at him too fast; the primary one that whatever Emma wanted, he wanted for her. She had never been unrealistic or unreasonable.

"I believe it can be a lovely room," she said. "It has two long windows that look west with a proper view of the garden. The room is well lighted; it catches the afternoon sun." Emma spoke enthusiastically as if this topic were already quite decided. "I believe the room receives enough heat, and there's a fireplace; Mr. Hobby may help himself to wood right outside the kitchen garden, and should that not be warm enough in winter, he can have use of a little heater. I don't think he should need that though." Emma's thoughts gained momentum. "There's even a bath; it must have been a butler's room once." Then she caught herself up and looked expectantly at Simon. She waited; she looked so hopeful.

During her appeal, Simon had been sitting, hand to chin, raised eyebrows in expectation for what she could come up with next. His heart warmed to her caring for this man. "But I say, Emma, how do you know so much about this room? We have so many rooms. I was born here and hardly know about it," he laughed. Emma was always a surprise to him.

"While looking for Schrödinger," she said, "I learned more about the manor then perhaps either you or Peter ever dreamed of knowing. Remember when Raíska locked Schrödinger in the security panel?"

"Ah, yes . . . we all felt panicky that evening, so bazaar for him not to show up on his tower for dinner."

"Right, and the next day, while looking for him, I found a few new rooms. And this one is begging for an occupant."

Without breaking down his different thoughts on the subject, Simon simply said, "My dear, I'm sure Mr. Hobby would be a good addition to the manor. We could have Agent Collins look into his past. However, I feel certain he would find nothing more than that unfortunate law suit."

So, on the spot, it was decided that Mr. Hobby would be offered the room, and Mrs. Penrose, the housekeeper, would assure that the room was presentable and contained whatever it had lacked: bed, dresser, desk and chair, carpet, lamp, bookcase, and linens—all of it. Moreover, to make the offer to Mr. Hobby acceptable, Emma was to plead that security for the ground floor was a dire necessity; they needed his help and they wanted someone they knew.

"You could study and read in peace, Mr. Hobby," Emma said while urging the offer and the request.

And that is the manner in which the manor accepted another person into its midst. Mr. Horace Hobby accepted the position with all seriousness; at night, in his new home, listening to every sound for possible breech of security. He had laughed when Emma warned him about the manor's ghost, Lady Joan, and about a pet cat, Schrödinger, both of whom enjoyed prowling around the manor, and both of whom, being unnaturally curious, might pay him a visit.

"A ghost?" he asked. "What am I to expect of her?"

"Nothing, really; she's quite benevolent," said Emma. "You might see her . . . she also prowls at night."

And when, on Mr. Hobby's first night in his new home, Lady Joan appeared just off the foot of his bed to inspect the new arrival, he stood his ground, and closing his robe more tightly around himself, he managed to contain his nerve. With a slightly tremulous voice he said, "Hello, Lady Joan. Pleased to make your acquaintance." Then, while he waited—frozen by half—Lady Joan did the polite thing and vanished. It took Mr. Hobby rather serious thinking to know whether he preferred these ghostly visits, or his damp, cramped automobile. Tonight, though, he was determined to be warm and dry in *this* bed, in *this* room, before the fire, ghost or no ghost.

On the next morning, as Mr. Hobby was moving his books and things from his car to his room, Emma asked him to come into the kitchen with her for a proper introduction to Mrs. Ogilvy and her staff.

"It's rather fine to have a man around, Mr. Hobby," Mrs. Ogilvy said. She knew nothing about the man, but she could see by his appearance that he could use a few squares. "Please feel free to visit with us when you want company . . . in fact, we would enjoy your company at meals. We're too used to Brooks and Hadley and the rest of the staff," she smiled. "You might entertain us whilst we snap beans. Watch out though, we may put you to work." She felt bold to address him so, but his manner appeared to be pleasantly accessible—in agreement with her offer.

A while later that day, Hadley appeared with the family's request for Mr. Hobby to join them above stairs for dinner. Horace declined, saying that Mrs. Ogilvy had already asked him to join the staff for dinner in the kitchen, and, finding himself looking forward to the first dinner to which he had been invited in over a year, he had agreed. He looked forward to that, and to Mrs. Ogilvy's pretty face. And he had felt the genuine, inviting warmth of her smile: something that would hold up, not disappoint.

19

Every day, every morning, afternoon and evening, Simon and Emma felt anew their delight and good fortune to be together. A miracle had occurred. Even though the threat on his life had not been entirely removed, Simon continued his Parliament work: that work for which Russian assassins wanted him dead or alive. He would not abandon that effort. In the long run it was critical for his country's safety. As well, he took certain risks at times to walk about with Emma; however, the manor was remote and it would be hard for someone with evil intentions to be around without being seen, no place close by to hide.

Emma had told Simon about his obituary and about the monument they had erected for him. He laughed over the obituary, saying, "Of course he mentions you and Peter, and even Lady Claire . . . I'll tell that gentleman to leave her out . . . but upon my soul, he has said nothing about Lady Joan and her importance to us, stirring things up. Still, it is awakening to read one's own obituary. There must be numerous articles round about now with the word, 'deceased' after my name."

Emma laughed at him. She found that these days laughter came more easily to her, and to the manor, and to Simon. "You think your obituary is remarkable, wait until I show you your monument. Not many people, perhaps no one, has a monument erected in his name whilst he's still alive. Come." She drew him toward the monument that she, Peter, and John Britely had put in place to honor Simon's life, to remember him until the end of time, and to help keep him in their hearts. When they reached the monument, Emma felt the seriousness of it, the memory of that day, and she worked to withhold tears.

Simon studied the monument, a large granite stone that said, "Here lie the remains of Lord Simon Appleby Haversham, Fifth Earl of Cav Neumont. Beloved of all." Below that were dates and testimony to his service for his country. Simon was sober for a minute; the monument would endure many millennia, and said "here lie," when actually here he stood, quite alive, studying his own monument. He thought about how he had missed the bomb that had taken two of his countrymen. That was sobering indeed. Hardly something in which to find humor. He was silent for a minute, then led Emma away. "Thank you my love. I am blessed beyond belief that I am still here for you."

20

Corky was pleased to find Edward seated at The Bucket. There he was, looking at her coming in the door as though he had been waiting for her.

"Good evening, my dear," he said, his hand reaching out to her. "I hoped you would come in. I haven't seen you in a while."

"Well, that's your own fault, isn't it? I've been here every evening, haven't I?"

"I had to be in Oxford," he lied, "and couldn't get back." Of course it was not for her to know about meetings with his Russian handlers. "And you know, I live in Craig-on-Wold, so the first thing on my list when I return, is grocery shopping and laundry. Living alone, I have all the chores to myself." He offered her the warmest smile hoping she would forgive him, for he had something important to press on her. First, he must warm her up, flirt a little, make her think he had missed her, and might even be open to an affair. He wasn't certain how she would react. Though it was plain that she enjoyed flirting, he had had no indication she meant it seriously, or wanted to take it further. And although he noticed Barney's stare, he took Corky's hand and held on to it.

Corky as well noticed that when Edward took her hand, Barney stared. And Barney knew Troy—was Troy's friend. Before Troy had begun all that studying, he had often come to The Bucket, sat at the bar and swapped stories with Barney.

"Let's sit outside for a while," Edward said. "It's warm enough and quite dry for a change."

"Good idea."

He held her arm while her short legs stepped down from the stool. She led him out of the tavern. They settled on a bench, and although the air was slightly chilly, and although the evening was beyond twilight, a gentle saffron glow, reluctant to leave the sky, pushed through the trees that were just leafing out in a larger way, and from all around village lights were warming in their own manner.

Edward said, "It's not as warm as I thought," and he moved closer to Corky snuggling her under his arm. "I have missed you," he said as he closed his arms more firmly around her.

They sat like that for a while. Corky bloomed within his embrace. It had been some time since she had felt the warm, strong arms of an attractive man. He began to nuzzle her neck.

"I wish there were some place we could be alone, completely alone together," he said. "Isn't there a room in the manor to which we could sneak, unbeknownst to anyone? Are there still people working in the kitchen?"

Corky could hardly believe what she heard. It would be so nice to continue this; his arms felt so good, she would like to feel his entire body. For a moment she thought—what to do? She pictured the couch in the kitchen where the cooks could rest for a few minutes; rest their tired feet.

"Don't you have a key to the rear entrance?" Edward asked.

"I do," she said, "For I'm usually the first one there each morning." Was this an admission that she would take him there? She knew on the moment, that was where they were headed. She stood, still holding his hand, and led him to the parking area where the golf cart waited. With the evening holding its breath for what was to come next, a few late birds softly calling goodnight, she drove Edward to the manor, questions and expectations mounting in the minds of each. As they bounced along the four-mile road, Corky thought how daring was what she was about to do. She hungered for this man. Hungered for his embrace. Passed that, she had not given a thought other than to dim the lights of the cart as they approached the manor.

She recalled that Tyler would be moving to a flat at the manor to establish security systems, but that was not to be concerned about now, for she did not think the man had yet made his moved. And although Mr. Hobby had moved in, his room was quite a way down the hall from the kitchen. Their main concern would be to arrive and steal in silently, for Mr. Hobby's room had windows at the rear. Thinking ahead, she believed that she and Edward would likely have all the privacy they could want.

When they reached the manor, Corky drove the cart around, not to the usual spot outside the door that led up to hers and Troy's flat, but further around back where she could park it unseen in complete darkness, where no one would venture. With its battery power, the cart was silent, and Corky had no worry about its being heard. Security lights would be lighted soon, but not as far back as she parked; no one would see them. She led Edward through the kitchen garden and to the rear entrance where she used her key, opened the door and preceded him in. Edward watched while she quickly pushed off the security alarm. Then he flashed around his light to see that they were moving through an old-fashioned mudroom filled with hanging herbs in various stages of drying.

"I'm sure all are in their rooms far upstairs," Corky said. "Except for Mr. Hobby. He's on this floor, but his room is down the hall. So we must be quiet."

"Mr. Hobby? Who's he?"

"Oh he's just someone who needed a place to live and they've given him a room in exchange for some service; not exactly sure about that."

Edward was concerned about the presence of a Mr. Hobby; he hadn't expected a Mr. Hobby, still, the man didn't appear to be up and about. All was as dark and as quiet as church mice. He was in it now and would continue; he had an order to find Lord Haversham.

"I'm curious," Edward whispered. "I've never seen a kitchen in a manor." Let her think he was curious, and as they entered the kitchen, he swept around his light, working to get his bearings. Then, as Corky proceeded to lead him, his light shined on a map on the wall to his right. "So this is how you find your way through the myriad of rooms and hallways."

"Not us cooks," Corky whispered, "We never go upstairs. That's for the butler and footman, though I 'spect they know what is where without the map."

She led him to the couch, and pulling him down, she cast her appeal up to his eyes. He doused his light, tucked it into his jacket pocket, and put his arm around her. She leaned completely into his arms, yielding up herself. But when he turned her head to kiss her, and when he began to caress her, she suddenly jerked away. She thought of Troy; she loved Troy; had been with him many years. What was she doing here while Troy was probably studying, trying to be a better man? Especially keen were the words Corky kept hearing that her ladyship had said to her that very morning: *Corky, we're quite pleased with Troy's work as docent.* Emma had stepped down to the kitchen, as she often did, to say hello to Mrs. Ogilvy and her staff. But in particular today, Emma wished to tell Corky that Troy had become an excellent docent. She had drawn Corky aside to speak to her in private: *Troy has surpassed our expectations, and we will be paying him well; he deserves it. And Corky, we hear good things about you. Mrs. Ogilvy is pleased with your work. Mr. Britely will be reviewing your pay as well.* This memory rose up fresh as if Lady Haversham stood there before Corky. Corky bolted to her feet.

"I've made a mistake. I can't do this," she said. She stood, took Edward's hand and pulled up the surprised man. She hoped he wouldn't turn violent, after all, she had tricked him, led him on, at least he might take it that way.

But Edward didn't mind at all: making love to this woman would have taken a supreme effort. He was more than happy to be released from the requirement, though he wouldn't show it lest he need this kind of situation in the future. He feigned disappointment.

"I understand, Corky. I hope there's another time. You are lovely to come to your decision as you have done." He used his flashlight to lead them toward the back door, and on the way, he shined his light on the wall map.

"Hold on a bit, Corky," he said. "Where is Lord Haversham's room . . . where he sleeps?"

"Oh, I wouldn't know. We don't have a need to know," she whispered. "Only Brooks and Hadley go anywhere beyond the kitchen. As you see the rooms are coded for simplicity."

Corky pulled Edward away from the map, and led him to the door. She set the security and the lock. Of course he let her go out first—the gentlemanly thing to do. And as he shut the door behind them, as Corky led the way to the golf cart, he flipped off the security and assured that the door was not closed completely. The reason for his entire evening, the entire venture, had been accomplished.

"I'm sorry," Corky said, "I'll drive you back to the village. It's late and you must drive to Craig-on-Wold."

"Thank you, my dear. It is late and I do have a lot of work waiting."

He didn't sound at all disappointed, Corky thought. Resilient. Should she mind, she wondered. Just the same, she would be happy to get home to Troy.

After Corky drove off, Edward Fitzpatrick waited a while to give her time to reach home. Then he used his mobile to summon help. He reviewed the directions for his men, Pyotr and Ilya, who would be along shortly in a battery-powered golf cart borrowed from The Meridian Inn. He would jog and walk the four miles, he said; meet them behind the manor. He started walking. He wouldn't use his car due to the noise. On the way, his men caught up to him. Wait for him in the shade far behind the manor, he explained, and when he reached the rear kitchen door, Pyotr and Ilya came out from the shadow where they had been waiting.

Listening to hear that all around the manor was quiet, with no one coming or going through the kitchen door, Edward motioned to Pyotr and Ilya for complete silence, and to follow him. He carefully, even slowly, opened the door, afraid that somehow the security had been reset to go on. But there was no sound. He crept in letting the two men follow. When they were inside the kitchen, Edward shined his light on the wall map. "This should show us which room is Lord Haversham's. They studied the various floors, hallways, and staircases but found it extremely confusing.

"Lord," Pyotr whispered in Russian, "this place is the size of a small town."

Most rooms were indicated with a few letters, such as 2DR, 3EH, 3ES, 3PH, and although the staff could make sense of it, it wasn't at all clear to strangers. They would have to take a risk; there wouldn't be many opportunities such as this to break in without sounding the alarm. "3EH," Edward whispered. "I suspect that's third floor east—'H' representing Haversham and I'm willing to try it. Now, make a mental note of the stairs and halls we should take to arrive at 3EH. It's on the east side. If we don't get twisted, we will be able to keep going east. Do either of you have a compass?" No one replied. "That's an omission. Well, keep your senses clear as to which direction is east. Now if we can just find that hallway." Pyotr and Ilya had remembered to carry a flashlight. And also AK-47's with silencers.

They started out of the kitchen moving silently along toward the left. There were too many hallways, making the map in their heads jingle. They hoped they could keep their bearings and Edward hoped that Mr. Hobby's room was far enough away that he couldn't hear any faint sound they might make. They had a sense that they were moving east and had started to relax, to gather confidence, when something tripped up Ilya's next step, causing him to fall and land hard with a loud crash onto his gun. The shock and extreme pain that went through him pushed out a yell that might have ricocheted throughout the entire manor had it not been so huge.

"Yow! Something tripped me," Ilya yelled. "Help me! My leg is broken! I can't move!"

Along with "Idiot! Are you crazy?" Edward swore at Ilya releasing a few Russian words not meant for the general public.

"You should feel what I felt! What tripped me?" Ilya cried as he lay there almost weeping. "I think you might have screamed also." And in crippling pain, he swore back similar Russian words.

Time was critical, and, leaving Ilya to fend for himself, Edward and Pyotr took off straight ahead, the light from their flashlights bobbing about. Hardened and toughened though they were, they now found themselves to be shaky. Whatever had tripped Ilya was an unknown: strange creatures could be here wandering around in the dark. What's more, in a rush to get away from whatever it was that hit Ilya, they had lost their bearings. They wildly flashed their lights about, but recognized nothing, not one hallway seemed to lead eastward. They were not quick enough to see Schrödinger fly down the hall to stairs, and up out of sight. Schrödinger had come down to nibble from his dish, but now he was on his way to sit outside Lord Haversham's door and yell. Something was going on that his lordship should know about. And although Schrödinger managed to trip up one intruder, it was too much to expect him to find all six legs at once.

"That's no way to treat an AK-47," Mr. Hobby calmly said. He stood over Ilya while he removed the gun from under the man. "Haven't they given you better training than this? *This* is the way to treat Kalashnikov," and he pointed the gun at Ilya. Mr. Hobby had awakened with the great clatter, and keenly feeling his role as guard, had pocketed his mobile and followed the commotion down the hall toward the kitchen, where he now held Ilya at gunpoint with Ilya's gun. As instructed, he phoned Agent Collins to report the break-in.

Now, with just the two of them, and completely lost, Edward was still determined to continue; it seemed less threatening to advance than to retreat. They crept forward until reaching a staircase. They went up and tried to continue in what seemed to be an easterly direction. If they could find windows where the moon could be seen, that would be east, but perhaps it was too late to catch the moon. Right. Any window would do. Actually anything would do, for, Edward thought, they might not be able to find their way out. And all this for Russia. Was Lord Haversham that important? They didn't know why, but someone in Russia wanted him out of the way, and they were the best men to move him there. Hearing no sound in any direction, and thinking they saw light coming from a window, they gathered courage and moved along more quickly. Finally, they came to a great hall studded with windows through which moonlight shown. It was almost as bright outside as during the day. So, Edward reasoned, they must find another staircase and go up another floor. He reasoned that a master suite would likely be a floor above the public rooms. He led Pyotr through the great hall and beyond, passing smaller hallways, until a staircase was in sight. They went up. The hallway at the top, except for moonlight shining through colored glass at one end, was almost completely dark. Edward sensed that they must be near Lord Haversham's room. And to offer proof, a cat was howling outside one of the doors. He had heard that that cat, when the earl was at dinner, would sit on a tower nearby to receive treats from him. This was Lord Haversham's room! Schrödinger let out a severe yell but stood his ground. Edward gestured to Pyotr to lunge at the door—it broke through.

Emma and Simon jerked up from under their covers to look down the barrels of two AK-47s.

But, before Edward and Pyotr could catch their breath, something buckled them to their knees. Gathering his wits Edward found enough strength to boldly stand and confront the force head-on. Pyotr took a firm stand directly behind Edward. They saw Lady Joan across the room, glowering at them. Edward hadn't time to remember that he was here to kill or capture Lord Haversham. Instead, he uttered a Russian swear, and said in English, "What in hell!" He could clearly see something strange across the room, but he was not in the mood to take Lady Joan seriously. He fired at her.

Edward would never remember what happened next, but as Emma and Simon witnessed, the gun's force turned on him, pushed him back through Pyotr, crashing the two men through the long French window with the small panes, dragging drapes along with them like a parachute, to land on a hedge three floors below.

They could hear a helicopter off in the distance. Neither Edward nor Pyotr thought of this as a time to linger, and coming untangled from drapes, brushing off themselves, pulling bits of hedge from their eyes, hair, and collars, hardly stalling long enough to know that they were bodily intact, they fled around back toward the kitchen entrance where the golf cart waited. There was no thought for Ilya's fate; no thought for trying to fetch him. Whatever Lord Haversham's worth to mother country, it counted for nothing this evening. They were ready to die of shock, their hearts dancing about irregularly. They sat for a bare moment, speechless, until they could breathe in enough oxygen to guide the cart around the manor and out down the road.

Except for Lady Joan who had retired to whatever place it was where she hung out, the entire manor household was astir and wondering what had happened. Simon had pulled the rope for help and Brooks, Hadley, and Pearce rushed to his side to see whether he and Lady Haversham were all right.

"What happened, my lord?" asked Brooks, his anxious face showed fear.

"We had visitors, and whatever they were after, they hadn't counted on finding Lady Joan. Two men, Brooks. Two men with AK-47s . . . powerless against Lady Joan. I do wonder how they entered the building without the alarm sounding. Please check the locks and security, Brooks. Don't I hear a helicopter?" Then he remembered Mr. Hobby. "I wonder whether Mr. Hobby is all right. Let's go down to check on him."

By the time Simon and Brooks arrived in the kitchen hallway, the helicopter, according to Mr. Hobby's instructions, had landed at the manor's rear, and Agent Collins and several commandos had taken over. They were holding Ilya until an ambulance arrived.

John Britely had thrown on his dressing gown and, following the commotion, had sped down the hall to Simon and Emma's room.

"We had visitors," Emma said. "Two men and when they met Lady Joan, they decided to leave. And in fact, they left in such a hurry, they took a shortcut out the window." She nodded toward the broken window. "Amusing how that harmless woman turns off some people. Simon and Brooks are downstairs checking on Mr. Hobby."

John smiled; he could relax. Simon and Emma were all right. "I'll pop down myself," he said. When he reached the kitchen level, he found a strange man lying injured on the floor.

"Ah, John, you missed the fun," Simon said.

"We're waiting for an ambulance, Mr. Britely," Agent Collins said. Having relieved Mr. Hobby he was holding Ilya at gunpoint. "And I've received a call to assure me that two other intruders have been caught down the road."

Other members of the staff stood nearby offering support in their own way. Despite the fear the intruders had caused, there was a sense that all was well.

"Just all in a day's work, John." Simon felt that he had been through a lot lately, might as well not get too excited about it. "You see, John . . . these men, knowing that my tombstone is already erected, and my obituary already publicized, cannot rest until they put paid to me."

By now, Emma, still shaking a bit, had come down and protectively enclosed her arms around Simon. He turned his face to hers and once more gave silent thanks.

In fair shape, despite their fall into a hedge, Edward and Pyotr had stumbled in the dark to the cart and sped it toward the village where their automobile waited. However, before they could reach the village, a team of commandos was waiting for them with a roadblock.

Edward and Pyotr came to a sudden stop. With thick hedges lining the narrow lane, there was no place to turn.

"Good evening," one of the commandos said. "We hope you mates have been having fun."

"There's another one of us back in the kitchen where we left him," Pyotr said. He wasn't going to let Ilya go free; Ilya would share their fate.

"Kind of you to let us know, mate. We're sure he'll want to accompany you."

After all the swapping back and forth of stories, and examining broken windows, sleep would not return this night for anyone at the manor; thoughts of AK-47s rang through tired heads.

21

It was a regular occurrence now for Mr. Hobby to have his meals with Mrs. Ogilvy and the staff, and he had become quite popular with each one. They wanted to hear all about his capturing Ilya, and he would always insist that Schrödinger had done the work. Mild natured, attentively listening to each of the staff, giving each absolutely courtesy, laughing at all jokes, sharing the knowledge he had gained as barrister—that if he happened to miss a day, due to business in London, or perhaps dining upstairs at Lady Haversham's insistence—then dinners in the kitchen would be unusually quiet. And when he would be back among them, joviality would reign again. The kitchen staff were a close group; except for Corky they had worked at the manor ten years or more, some quite more. With increasing mouths to feed including inside staff and outside staff, they worked a full day at this, and they throve on the community around the table at meals, each trying to top the rest with humor.

With a comfortable room, a safe, warm and dry sleeping place of his own where he could arrange his personalty and keep organized, Mr. Hobby's entire appearance began to change. First, he walked to the village and had a crisp haircut that allowed just enough left on sides so he could brush back his sideburns in the manner he preferred, and that allowed the silver he had acquired there to show. (And which, unknown to him, appealed quite a bit to Mrs. Ogilvy.) As well he had the barber treat him to a clean shave. Then, he took the one suit he had managed to save, to the drycleaners in the village. Thankful to have it, he hadn't appeared in it yet, intending to save it for certain occasions. For the rest of his clothing, scant though it was, he had use of the manor's washing machines and iron. He was fixing up. When he appeared now at dinner, he was no longer scruffy looking; on the contrary, he looked crisp and tidy. These changes occasioned much chirping and cajoling around the table at meals, which Mr. Hobby received with his classic good humor.

And he had a new friend: while checking out unusual manor situations, Major found Mr. Hobby. The Labrador remembered sitting by his feet at New Chance, and sometimes after Mr. Hobby had turned out his light, and settled into bed, he could hear Major at the door, begging to be allowed in. Mr. Hobby would welcome the dog, and soon, when Major joined Mr. Hobby, he found a plush dog bed waiting for him.

Mrs. Ogilvy—Heather was her given name—in particular took notice of the slow changes in Mr. Hobby. So as not to show, she released little side glances mostly to confirm her suspicion that Mr. Hobby was handsome. However, Mr. Hobby, now Horace (he had asked them please to refer to him as "Horace"), missed very little; twenty years he had been a barrister; twenty years his training had enabled him to read most faces, and he enjoyed knowing that Mrs. Ogilvy gave him particular attention of the personal kind.

Once the staff learned that he was an unemployed barrister, the questions began to flow. Only Mrs. Ogilvy held back. In addition, they listened fixedly to each word of his refined, courtly accent (they assumed he had picked it up in Court). Although, had they thought about it, it wasn't all that different from Mrs. Ogilvy's, and she hadn't been in

Court. Each would stare at Mr. Hobby when he spoke—hearing the musical quality of his replies. With his company at dinner, the staff found current news and politics to be more interesting than in the past and saved up topics and questions about which to discuss at meals when Mr. Hobby was there. Moreover, it pleased them that he preferred to join them for dinner than to dine upstairs with the family. Brooks assured them that he had several times heard Lady Haversham ask Mr. Hobby for his company at dinner. So Mrs. Ogilvy and staff knew it to be true—his preference for downstairs dinner. The staff, always treated with respect, felt a greater honor these days.

Ultimately though, it was that the charms of Mrs. Ogilvy outshone the charms of dining upstairs. Mr. Hobby increasingly enjoyed Mrs. Ogilvy's smile; that one meant especially for him, he thought. He found that he warmed to it, and began to look forward to dinners in the kitchen more than just for the excellent fare.

"Where did you learn your culinary skills, Mrs. Ogilvy?" He wanted to draw her out; wanted to learn something about her. Perhaps when she took a break, he thought he might ask her to walk about with him. He had seen from his window that on occasion she selected greens from the kitchen garden. He could ask her about the vegetables—who planted them? who tended the garden?

"I believe she was born with a skillet and wisp making brown sauce," Brooks said. "Was there ever a time, Mrs. Ogilvy when you didn't know how to cook?"

Her warm smile spread across the table and wrapped itself over all, but rather more on Mr. Hobby. "I was the oldest of four. Our father died whilst the youngest was a baby and growing up I was expected to help my mum with everything, including cooking. When I turned sixteen, I went to work in a restaurant to help pay my sisters' and brother's way through good schools, including university. Today they have good careers and I know almost everything there is to know about cooking. Besides, I could not do this without my competent assistants." She nodded around to her cooks. "After my siblings had earned their degrees, and I had learned enough about catering, baking, and all that, I went into service, and I would not leave this family, this manor. I had thought about opening a café, but I decided that I wanted to do special cooking for a few, rather than rushed cooking for many. Other than that I did not get an education."

"That's not true, Mrs. Ogilvy, you're self-educated," Corky said. "I've seen you studying something every chance you have."

Mrs. Ogilvy smiled at Corky. She was learning that Corky had a good inner character that just needed a bit of taming. Mr. Hobby was learning that Mrs. Ogilvy was a woman of distinction and integrity. Unobserved, he studied her, and thought about the new chances that had opened up for him because he had needed a cup of tea and a bun. *The mercy that droppeth like rain on all below.*

With lunch over, Mr. Hobby retired to his room to study. For over a year, he had been shut out of his profession as barrister, and although he had tried to keep up, studying in his cold, damp car had been slow going. Now he wanted to review, catch up on recent Court decisions and changes. And the large desk that Lord and Lady Haversham had so graciously provided, and the crackling fire made the task so pleasurable. And there each day he studied. As well, he read the newspapers that Brooks brought down for him.

At first, Brooks would bring down the family's paper when they had finished with it. But when Emma discovered this, she asked John Britely to add a subscription for Mr. Hobby. Thus, Mr. Hobby had his own copy straight away at breakfast.

"Brooks," he said when the butler first brought down a fresh copy, "please do not go to this trouble for me."

"Sir, Lady Haversham ordered this paper for you. She thought you should have your own copy."

Mr. Hobby could only stare at Brooks.

"That's the way she is, sir. Always thinking about someone's welfare and pleasure. It's pointless to object."

Early on, Mr. Hobby had worried about how he could repay the family who were so generous to him. He had already asked Mrs. Ogilvy to call him when she needed help in the kitchen—perhaps needed a stronger hand than that available among the cooks. In the past she would call Hadley; he was often down anyway to replenish the cooks' fire; the fire they could sit before whilst taking a tea break. Now, say if one of the cooks had to slice a pineapple, she would call on Mr. Hobby, usually in his room. With one whack of the tough fruit, he would halve it. Same for cabbages. Amazing the number of growing things that were hard to hack through. Mr. Hobby helped in such small ways, but he wanted to give more serious repayment for the luxury he felt himself now to be in.

"Mr. Hobby, kindly come upstairs and lend us your company for dinner this evening," Emma said. She had found him in the kitchen scrubbing out a cast-iron pot that had a thick layer of burnt cream welded on to it. Normally no one in the kitchen would allow something to burn, but Tina, one of the cooks, had had an unexpected phone call, and in her haste had left the pot unattended.

"Mr. Hobby! You are not to become a cook," Emma said. "We want you to resume your law profession, if and when you care to."

"Not to worry, Lady Haversham. I lend a hand here only on occasion; although I would gladly assist Mrs.

Ogilvy every day, would she allow it." And perhaps he hadn't intended to, but he offered Emma a knowing smile.

"Indeed, Mrs. Ogilvy is a national treasure, but do not tell anyone. Still, I say we would greatly benefit by having you dine with us. Our banal conversation needs an injection. Please do join us."

That evening about six, after Mr. Hobby bathed, he applied the tiniest dashed of Eau Sauvage, just a whiff—a personal item he had found at the barbers—donned his one and only fresh-out-of-the-cleaners suit, polished his go-to-Court shoes, and went in to talk to Mrs. Ogilvy and her staff.

"Dear Mrs. Ogilvy, he said, "I'm so sorry to be dining this evening without your good graces." He was happy to see her brow lift with a question. "But as you already know, I have been requested by higher powers to dine upstairs . . . I surmise they think you need a break from my wagging mouth and sagging jowls."

"Right," Mrs. Ogilvy said. "We complain in particular about your sagging jowls."

He continued as though what he had to say outweighed anything she had to say, "And I hope you plan to serve the same culinary treats for us upstairs, as you typically do here. Though I am aware that they don't deserve it as do we for providing our smartness to the kitchen dinners."

"Mr. Hobby," she said, "Rest assured . . . I'll be sending up peanut-butter and jelly sandwiches. Isn't that true, Tina?"

"Absolutely," said Tina as she stirred a béchamel in a large saucepan. "I'm just spreading the peanut butter now. And didn't you say you were sending up for Mr. Hobby a special can of Major's chow?" She had seen Major at Mr. Hobby's feet; the Labrador followed him whenever he could.

"And just for saying such nonsense, Mrs. Ogilvy, as well as allowing your cook to do the same . . . I compel you to walk about with me tomorrow . . . for one hour at least. I'll train you not to be so corny." And before his joking with her caused his face to become red, he spun on his highly-polished heels and swiftly strode out of the kitchen and up to the library where the family was gather.

Mrs. Ogilvy's gaze followed him out the door. She would miss him at dinner tonight. It wouldn't be quite as much fun as it could be, and most likely she wouldn't see him again until morning.

"Mrs. Ogilvy," Tina said, "I think you have caught an admirer just as surely as if you had cast out a line and hook." It was fairly certain that Mr. Hobby had snared Mrs. Ogilvy as well, Tina wanted to say, but thought better of it.

"You do say silly rubbish," said Mrs. Ogilvy as she turned away laughing.

The family had gathered in the library for sherry and were waiting for Lord Haversham to take his seat. He was studying shelves of books, all of which had a serious, heavy appearance. He pulled down a few and placed them on a table near Mr. Hobby, where he sat, sherry in hand, around the fire with Emma, Hannah and John.

"Let us toast Mr. Hobby," Emma said. "He has so completely won over our kitchen staff. I hear from Brooks, that should he wish, Mr. Hobby could open up his own manor and straight away carry them all off."

Mr. Hobby merely smiled. "Please call me 'Horace,' " he said, petting Major who was spread out near his chair.

"And see," said Emma, "he's won over our dog. Mr. Hobby . . . Horace . . . I believe Major must be staying nights in your room, for we don't see him in the evening lately."

"Well," Mr. Hobby began, "the mysterious appearance of a plush dog bed may have had something to do with that. I vow I am innocent."

"Indeed, you are innocent," Simon broke in. "On a serious note," he continued, "I've been doing some research into your unfortunate case." He pointed to the books on the table. "You know all about these . . . but you're welcome to scan them to review, should you want to."

"Sir Simon," Mr. Hobby said, "the problem is that my solicitor won to have the critical files sealed. I needed those files to support my case . . . that before the Court I argued incorrect facts. My solicitor had provided me with incorrect facts. Indeed false."

"Yes. Quite so," Simon said. "But figuring that my time spent helping the Cabinet ought to be good for something, I asked for a favor. And just today I have succeeded in acquiring an order to have them unsealed. Uncertain whether I would be successful, I have withheld mentioning this to you before now . . . you have access to your files."

Except for the fire's gentle crackling, there was complete silence in the room while all waited for Mr. Hobby's response. He looked as though he were in a different universe, not comprehending what was occurring in this one. He struggled for belief, and for what exactly to say. He had never had hope of accessing the sealed files; doing so would require internal influence and intervention at the highest level of government.

"Why, sir!" he said, after Sir Simon's meaning finally registered in his soul. Even the quiet room, it seemed, waited for more from Mr. Hobby, but this was his entire speech.

"The files will be available for you tomorrow in Lord Tewk's chambers. He's holding them for you. If you like, Hadley will drive you to the train, so you won't have to worry about parking."

Mr. Hobby's sherry glass fairly trembled in his hand. "I don't know how to thank you, sir."

"So, do not try. Save your energy for concentrating on winning back your excellent reputation."

Brooks announced dinner, and they moved through to the dining room, and silently took their seats. No one could think of what to say that would sound normal while knowing that Mr. Hobby was choked with emotion. After a while, though, the sound of clicking forks was overtaken by Mr. Hobby's try at humor. "Mrs. Ogilvy said she was sending up a peanut-butter and jelly and some of Major's chow for me. I must mention to her how unreliable she can be."

"I see," said Emma, "that Mrs. Ogilvy has won you over in her own way. Welcome to the manor, Horace."

"Do you think Mr. Hobby is organizing an appeal?" Emma asked Simon. They were about to turn in for the night. As the moon journeyed to the west, the soft outline of the manor shadowed itself across the terrace and field. Emma stood before the open French window letting her peignoir drift around her lithe form. On these lovely evenings, she liked to feel the warm breeze that wanted to touch down inside. Simon watched her loveliness, his breath held in fascination. She turned to catch his answer and then he remembered her question. He stepped over to her and enclosed her in his arms. Together they looked out onto the shadowed terrace.

"I don't think he can pay for an appeal," Simon finally answered. "As I understand it, he was completely wiped out after leaving a settlement on his estranged wife . . . nothing left but a pittance. I've looked into it, listened to some gossip in London, and it is truly a scandal. I'd like to help him. That means offering him financing so he can win in Court. That takes funds that I feel he won't accept. Even so, we can offer him a loan, payable after he's again earning."

"Do help him, Simon. He's such a pleasant, fellow, and one senses his frustrated intelligence and training just waiting to burst forth; I want so to see him succeed."

"But just how to make the offer . . . he is of course, quite proud."

"Indeed, I can't fathom how that might be done. Unless you simply come right out with it. He feels his need, acutely, and would likely succumb more easily to a direct approach."

They were silent while they thought about Mr. Hobby's plight.

"Yes. That's what I must do," said Simon. And he went to bed debating with himself various approaches to helping Mr. Hobby financially. The next day he asked Brooks to kindly summon Mr. Hobby. "Ask him, if he is free, to please join me for coffee after dinner. Tell him I have something to discuss. Ask him to come to my study."

After Mr. Hobby greeted Simon and took a seat, and after Brooks poured their coffee and left the room, Simon began. He had been pacing the room, still mentally arranging the best way to present his offer so Mr. Hobby could accept it.

"Mr. Hobby, I must make you an offer that you are not allowed to refuse; not until your case has been won, at which time you may then refuse it." He smiled at Mr. Hobby hoping to remove the man's serious, fearful look, so embattled he had been, that Simon wanted to hasten—to rush his offer—to relieve the man.

"In order to file and complete your case, you will need substantial finances. We . . . Lady Haversham and I . . . are offering that to you, and when you win, you may return it to us; consider it a loan."

A jolt of sorts, leaving him unprepared for speech, went through Mr. Hobby as he tried to take in this offer. It was true that due to lack of funds, even after gaining access to the pertinent files, he would have to drop the case before it got to Court. Nothing could be said that would adequately show his astonishment at Simon's offer.

"I know that you can represent yourself in Court," Simon went on, "not be required to hire a barrister, your being the best there is . . . nevertheless you need a financial kick-start."

Mr. Hobby tried to steady himself, his emotions, by sipping coffee, but his hand, just a mite, did tremble. "To say 'thank you' to you and Lady Haversham, can hardly convey my appreciation. It's quite true that I have been unsure how to proceed; whether I *could* proceed."

Simon wanted to conclude this embarrassing discussion. "Mr. Hobby, I'll immediately issue a bank credit for you to draw on. Consider it done, and this shall remain completely private between you, Lady Haversham, and me."

That night, when he and Emma were alone, Simon told her about his success with his offer to Mr. Hobby. "He had nowhere else to go. And I feel he is quite deserving. We had to do this."

"Exactly. Simon, I admire your instincts." There was a long pause between them. "I love you for your instincts."

"And I you for yours," he replied.

As their eyes closed for sleep that night they felt something important had begun that would yield a fruitful future for someone quite deserving. Someone they were able to help.

Coming down from his meeting with Simon, Mr. Hobby found the kitchen dark when he looked into it for Mrs. Ogilvy. All of the kitchen staff had gone up to their rooms on the fourth floor. He would have to postpone his talk with Mrs. Ogilvy and must turn in without telling her goodnight. And on the next day he would be off early for the trip into London to pick up crucial documents. With funds from Sir Simon and Lady Haversham, he now saw his way to forming an appeal. The money had been near on to impossible to accept, but he had confidence he could win his case and be rewarded his absconded wealth. Before going down the hall to his room—Major following, he took a piece of notepaper from the kitchen log and wrote a note for Mrs. Ogilvy:

"Missed saying goodnight.
For the next few days, I
must be in London.
Horace."

In the morning it was Tina who found Mr. Hobby's note. He had left it on the middle worktable for all to see, and when Mrs. Ogilvy came into the kitchen, Tina waved the paper at her until she came over to see what Tina had. As Mrs. Ogilvy read the note, she felt its intention to speak directly to herself. "He's a lovely man," she said, a smile spreading over her face, "and we as well have grown used to his company. We'll miss him."

"Right . . . some of us more than others," Tina's suggestive grin caused Mrs. Ogilvy to flush.

"I'll miss his jokes," said Mrs. Ogilvy.

"Sure . . . his jokes!"

"You know that he's a barrister . . . used to dealing with serious problems. And yet he can sit here with us and be as corny sometimes as the rest of us. He adds to our levity."

"Why is he living here with us, Mrs. Ogilvy, and seems to have no sign of a career?"

"I don't know the story, but I think he was sued and lost everything."

"You mean we could have a crook living amongst us?"

"Not likely! The Havershams trust him and that's good enough for me."

It did not seem normal to Mr. Hobby to be going in to bed without having a word with Mrs. Ogilvy. He missed her cap, always covering her pinned up hair. He surprised himself by thinking that he wanted to see her hair down once; he never had, though an occasional stray told him that her hair was dark blonde with wisps of white. Fortunately, she couldn't cover those green eyes. Interesting that with critical files now available—files that could clear his name and return his wealth—he was instead thinking about Mrs. Ogilvy.

Before she turned out her light, Mrs. Ogilvy lay in bed reading. She would read one sentence and try to absorb that, before an image of Mr. Hobby would overlie it. More's the pity, she thought, they came from different backgrounds. But did they come from different cultures, she wondered. And he would solve his professional problem—she could sense that—and he would move on. Even though he had comfortable accommodation here—she knew that he would not long live on the kitchen level of Cav Neumont Manor. Clearly he belonged upstairs, belonged at their dining table. She knew, had overheard, Lady Haversham ask him on occasion to dine with them, and had heard him decline. He seemed to want to keep his original place as it had begun at the manor. She felt that he admired her more than just a casual admiration. She hoped that he didn't leave them too soon. He *would* leave—of that she was certain.

Normally when Mrs. Ogilvy took a break and walked out, she would think about her grocery list, or food combinations, recipes, that sort of thing. Or, she would stroll through the vegetable garden to see how the crops were coming along: decide whether it was time to plant more bush beans; admire the pole beans just beginning to rise up the poles that the gardeners had lovingly set in. Or she would examine the organized rows of supports for tomato plants. But lately this garden admiration lay in the background of her thoughts, for she continued to focus on Mr. Hobby. He had instructed everyone to refer to him as Horace, but she and the other cooks felt uncomfortable doing so, and continued to call him Mr. Hobby. Mrs. Ogilvy was used to gentlemen; one sister married to a surgeon—one to a journalist, and her brother situated in finance. However, with her own social life rather constrained, she had become unused to society. She hadn't missed it, had thrived on her life as it was; enjoyed its simplicity. But this strange happening—Mr. Hobby coming to live with them had opened up new ideas, new sensations.

Mr. Hobby spent three days in London successfully reviewing the pertinent files that his former solicitor had misrepresented to him causing him to argue false information before the Court. He had formed a plan and would appeal to the Court, asking for the return of all his funds, as well as for damages. For this he stayed another three days drawing up his claim which he then submitted to the High Court. When he returned home—that is back to his room at Cav Neumont Manor—his sense of optimism was unbounded, and when he first saw Mrs. Ogilvy, he grabbed her and danced around the kitchen. all the cooks clapping.

"Mr. Hobby!" Mrs. Ogilvy said after he released her. "How you do go on! I take it that your trip to London was quite successful."

"Uncertain. But I feel encouraged. Extremely important files had been sealed, and with a bit of help and encouragement from Lady Emma and Sir Simon, I won the right to have them unsealed: the first step. Their information is my entire case, and I have filed it with the High Court. However, I'm looking at another year, or more, to have my day in Court." He looked around at all the cooks and said, "And meanwhile I'll have the sarcasm and unbelievable jeers of all your cooks to keep me on my toes." He had a way of bringing laughter that the kitchen workers had indeed missed, and now they provided him with that sarcasm, but they kept it soft, having truly missed the man.

Tina thought he should know. "Mr. Hobby," she said. "Now all our sauces will be smooth, and none of our meats will be burnt. Nothing seemed to work out right in your absence."

"Exactly," someone else said. "I had noticed that and wondered what the cause was. Now I understand . . . Mr. Hobby's voodoo was missing."

The first thing on Mr. Hobby's mind after he unpacked and freshened up, was to have a quiet conversation with Mrs. Ogilvy, and if possible, a long walk with her. He had missed her. With his possibly living once more in London, and with her preference for her life at the manor, he had no idea where this connection would take either of them, but that was not to worry about now; just to do the immediate thing and have a bit of her company.

"Mrs. Ogilvy, would you kindly take a walk with me to the vegetable garden? I saw from my window that it looks inviting and I wish to see what's coming along. As I've lived so long in London without a vegetable garden, I won't recognize the young plants . . . when you have a chance, of course."

"I have a chance right now." She might be nervous but might as well get over this, not put it off. She did want to be with him in some way. "How did your London work go, Mr. Hobby?" she asked as they approached the rows of vegetables. He had already given a brief explanation, but

146

she found it difficult to have ready words to settle her nervousness.

"If you don't call me Horace, I'll make your sauces curdle, Mrs. Ogilvy."

"Then I insist that you call me Heather." She realized how close together that would seem to bring them.

"That'll feel odd for a while, Heather. But only for a while. I fancy that name, by the way. As for my work in London, I'll have my day in Court, but the outcome is unknown. With your help, and with the good emanations from the kitchen, I'll be optimistic." Although he had a good idea what they saw, what was growing where, they needed simple topics to discuss and he encouraged Mrs. Ogilvy—Heather—to talk about the garden, point out what was important for their summer dishes, as well as for canning. And at the end of that walk, they were comfortably "Heather" and "Horace," with each looking forward to future private walks and talks.

One day, Tina said, "I heard that Mr. Hobby was completely cleaned out and had been living in his car. Thus, I wonder how he affords his trips to London. And how will he afford a court case?" She looked at Mrs. Ogilvy with her question.

"I have no idea, my dear, but I expect that he did have some money put aside for emergencies." Mrs. Ogilvy had other ideas about how he was being funded, but it was not her business to suggest such ideas.

Each day that Mr. Hobby had no business in London, he tried to meet the manor staff for meals. It had become a looked-forward-to occurrence. Nevertheless, he missed his tea days at New Chance and so one day with favorable weather, he decided to walk the four miles to the village, browse about, and once again have tea at New Chance. When he arrived, he saw that Emma and Lady Mardling were the volunteers, and he hoped that one of them would take a minute to sit with him. Emma, helping a customer, caught a quick glance at him and remarked to herself how happy he looked—so different from when she first met him. Lady Mardling had not yet seen him in his spruced up person and was required, though she knew better, to stare at him. Remembering herself she quickly turned back to a customer, but thought about Mr. Hobby's clean-shaven face, smart attire, and his look—that was what had caught her so—he *looked* successful, not as the cast-down man before. She knew that he had moved to the manor with the stipulation that they needed ground-floor security, but still she was surprised at his transformation.

"We wish you would have dinner with us more often," Emma said. She had taken a break to sit with him. "Although we are an eager, gossipy group at dinner, times we find ourselves tired of our same, what can be . . . banal . . . company. Please do come add variety to our sameness, Mr. Hobby."

As always on his talks and tea with Emma, he would decline saying, "But, they are ever so much more banal in the kitchen and have come to need my company to keep them on their toes supplying those gourmet meals I've enjoyed at your table. I'm afraid that Heather . . . ," (whoops he had meant to say, Mrs. Ogilvy), "Mrs. Ogilvy," he corrected himself, "has grown used to my encouragement. And just the other day she called on me to cut apart a stubborn cabbage. I hope to earn my keep not only as watchman, but by cutting apart cabbages as well." He thought it best to leave out the part describing his and Heather's sitting at night, before the kitchen fire, swapping stories. While Heather would make hot chocolates, he would bring in firewood, and stoke up the fire that had burned throughout the day. Besides, though Lady Haversham could not know it, he always looked forward to his meals with Heather Ogilvy: too much information for Lord and Lady Haversham.

Emma understood. Then, for a moment, the air between them listened for what was next.

"Mr. Hobby . . . we'll wait for your timing." She knew that he keenly felt the benefit of his room at the manor, and did not want to overstep his presence there.

Although it was normally the case that appeals to The High Court—with much back-and-forth between the clerks, defense, and prosecutor, with their efforts to settle the case out of court, with efforts at mediation—would in fact take a year or more, Lord Haversham, had no thought of allowing Mr. Hobby to suffer that long without compensation. He felt he could straighten the curves; he had his connections and there were those who owed him a favor, and now he would call for one. He soon found an opportunity to present the facts to an acquaintance who happened to be a High Court Judge. Over dinner at Lord Haversham's club, he showed his friend the evidence that a former Judge had not had access to, or had ruled inadmissible. This allowed his friend to see that otherwise, Mr. Hobby would not have lost his case, and now must win his appeal so he could clear his name and get back to work in his profession.

Thus it was that within three months Mr. Hobby's appeal had its day before a High Court Judge. With his files unsealed, and without German backing, the defending solicitor knew his position was weak, and he would not join in mediation. This further weakened his case, and the decision went in Mr. Hobby's favor. He was awarded all his lost funds plus damages for the time he had suffered: for losing his home, his wife, everything. Mr. Hobby left Court in a stupor. All the way back to Cav Neumont—and he did certainly want to reach Cav Neumont that day—he hardly knew what to think. In fact he could not think, his mind nearly a blank now with only one idea: compensation after more than a year's deprivation. Finally, he realized he was bubbling over, had to tell someone, tell someone who cared about him, he had to be in Cav Neumont Manor.

And that evening extraordinary celebrations were carried on, both upstairs and in the kitchen. Mr. Hobby was up and down, and on both floors sherry flowed and little congratulatory speeches were offered up for him.

"Mr. Hobby," Lord Haversham said, "with this Court decision, your good name has most certainly been restored, and each time I am in London, I will loudly boast about your success to anyone who will listen, that you were innocent, and defamed in a shameful manner."

Mr. Hobby, with his usual reserve, almost felt it to be unlucky should he boast, and he did not. He merely sipped his sherry, then said: "Thank you, sir. And thank you and Lady Haversham for all your support. I've opened a bank account, several in fact, for part of my funds are to be forthcoming immediately. I am eager to repay you. That's foremost in my thoughts." He had more to say— about which he must think: too much for this evening.

What he wanted to say, or rather to ask, was whether he could stay on in his room. With all the terrorists having been caught, the Havershams might not feel a need for him to act as watchman. He wanted to say that he wouldn't be starting up his practice immediately. Enough for tonight though, he would discuss that tomorrow if he could.

And one might think that joy reigned about both up and down, and mostly that was true, but there were two people who weren't sure just how to feel. Namely, Mr. Hobby, who mulled over the prospects of moving back to London to begin his practice, moving away from his comfortable room at the manor, not walking the gardens regularly, not having meals with Heather. Heather. Not having meals with Heather? That would be unthinkable, practice notwithstanding. And so sleep took its time to fall in place for him.

Could he but know that Heather Ogilvy was under the same influence—sleep taking a stand-off whilst she mulled over Mr. Horace Hobby's moving back to London, leaving the manor for good. She was pleased with his success in Court, happy for him, and surely he would be back for visits, but my word, she thought, how awful that would be—not to see him more than that, not to hear the laugh she had grown so use to, not to see his spruce smiling face, his cheerful self—even after he had been living a year and more with adversity and disappointment. Not to have him at meals—insupportable. And yet she had to think it.

"Sir Simon, perhaps you and Lady Haversham no longer need my help with security. Still, I ask whether I might stay on a bit whilst I get my bearings." Mr. Hobby spoke to Simon before dinner. Simon and Emma had urged him up to dine with them so they could continue to bathe in his success. And, he could hardly say no, so there he was having sherry with them before dinner. His plea was not so much for himself; well perhaps it was—he wasn't eager to move away from Heather, but that was private information.

"As well, the bulk of my award won't come in immediately," he continued. "And although I have received a small portion for living expenses, I'm not in a rush to return to London. If it doesn't inconvenience you, perhaps just for a while, you could accept me as a tenant. I've enjoyed your gardens so, I want to slowly transition to the noise and traffic of London; start my practice up slowly."

"Tenant?" In his thoughts, Simon paused at the word tenant. That reminded him that Firefly Cottage would soon fall empty, for Lady Claire, who leased it now, would be moving permanently to Craig-on-Wold to join her friend, Oliver. Simon had absolutely no wish to relocate Mr. Hobby, but perhaps Mr. Hobby had tired of his ground-floor room. Thus, when he could find a good pause in Mr.

Hobby's request he said, "Mr. Hobby, you've met the former Lady Haversham, Claire."

"Yes. At New Chance. The window designer."

"Right. Lady Claire is moving to Craig-on-Wold to join her partner. She has been leasing Firefly Cottage, and it will be empty. I'm absolutely not urging you to leave the manor . . . no . . . it has always been our pleasure to have your company, but you are welcome to lease Firefly. It's fairly secluded, tucked back; you probably have not seen it. But a short walk from here, it has a lovely garden."

Mr. Hobby had a puzzled look, another surprise, more change; change on top of change. He had been dimly aware of the cottage, barely peeking through the woods, hiding its existence.

"We urge you to stay here as long as you wish, forever as it were. You are a good addition to the manor. I only offer the cottage in case you aren't ready to move to London, and yet would like more space and privacy. And, as well, it's important for Firefly to have a caring occupant."

Privacy! Mr. Hobby thought he had all the privacy he needed at the manor; no one invaded his room, and it had a lovely view, and was quiet. And he could walk down the hall to the kitchen. Heather was usually in the kitchen.

"Sir Simon," Mr. Hobby said, "Might I wait to decide when my funds actually arrive; I believe they expected ten days. I want to give some thought to what I should do first. I have so much to think about." And beyond his control, thinking about Heather Ogilvy seemed to be at the top of the list. What could he do about Heather? If anything.

Mrs. Ogilvy wasn't as exuberant these days as formerly, although Mr. Hobby continued to join them for meals, and continued to ask her to walk with him. He said he wanted to talk about the ending of spring vegetables, the middle of summer ones, and the beginning of those for fall. He wanted her to tell him about the yellow blossoms ready to open in a large plot. What were they going to be? She pointed out some buds, now about the size of a golf ball, and said they were becoming squash and pumpkins, and one plant would be Hubbards. With the pumpkins she would make soup, bread, pies, and she didn't yet know what would become of the Hubbards, but they were lovely to look at. She walked with him without the light-heartedness as before; that knowledge always in the background that he soon would leave. Might as well get it out there, she thought.

"Mr. Hobby," she said. "Horace . . . when are you to leave us and start your work in London?"

He waited long minutes before finding his answer. He was qualified to present a case in the highest Court, but unable to voice his answer for Heather. This was the most sensitive question he had had in dozens of years, and his answer—if he weren't mistaken he could hear it coming— might be one of Heather's most surprising. Before he spoke he pinched off a few brown leaves from squash plants.

While she waited for his reply, she walked around to the other aisle to pinch off more.

"Heather, the Havershams have offered me Firefly Cottage . . . you know . . . the one that first Sophia and now Lady Claire have leased. Lady Claire is moving into her friend's place in Craig-on-Wold. I think it will be good to take the cottage until my practice is established again, that will take time, and I've hardly started. I don't have to be in London every day, and can work quite well from Firefly. The Havershams seem to think that I might need my own place. But as well, they don't want the cottage left empty, and would rather have a tenant they know."

"Oh."

He looked across the squash plants to her; she looked uncertain, even troubled. He wished her face would brighten up. "But, Heather, it's an easy walk to join you for meals."

Yes, that's true, she thought, but not the same as having you coming and going about during the day; not as easy to join you for walks, or to sit before the fire at night, talking. It wouldn't be the same. Would, in fact, be less than the same. Much less.

He saw her face grow long and form pockets of sadness that she tried to conceal.

"Come," he said, reaching out for her hand. "On your day off, I want to take you out to dinner."

She took his hand across the garden aisle and let him have a smile. What was to be would be, she thought, enjoy every minute.

22

Mr. Hobby, I've received a call for you." Emma had walked down to the kitchen to find him at a kitchen table jostling papers about. "You have a message from Mrs. Alice Hobby. Here's her number . . . she wants you to ring her." Although it wasn't her business, Emma wondered whether this was Horace's former wife, the woman who left him when he lost everything.

"Indeed . . . that's odd. I wonder how she found me here." He looked over at Heather, working nearby. He had purposely brought his research into the kitchen where she had cleared a space for him to work. He liked being near her, and she didn't go on chattering; nor did the other cooks; left him able to think. Now he felt wounded, the information that his former wife had called brought back sad memories. And for some reason he felt guilty on Heather's behalf.

Heather gave him a quick glance then made certain not to appear curious. She didn't see him shrug his shoulders, as though to say don't ask me, I haven't seen or called her.

"Until recently . . . since I lost that case, and lost my townhome . . . I haven't had an address or a listed mobile. I hope she isn't in trouble of some kind, and I certainly hope

she isn't after money; she was paid before anyone else. I'll give her a call." And that was all he said about it that day.
For the next days no one heard whether he had called his former wife, or heard anything about her. Mrs. Ogilvy wondered though. She felt heavy with wonder.

"I would love to see you. I have missed you," the former Mrs. Alice Hobby said to Horace Hobby over the phone. Putting it off for a day, he had finally made the call to learn what she wanted. He had no feelings for her. Still he didn't wish her harm, and if she were in a dire situation, though he would loathe to be involved, he would help her. They had been married twenty years, and he hadn't blamed her for wanting out when he lost the court case, and subsequently, to settle damages, lost everything else. All through the case, he had been so strained, so tied up with worry and confusion that he had not been there for her; had hardly been a husband. He had risen early, had gone off to his chambers or to Court, had arrived home late depressed and in a state of disbelief, had barely spoken to anyone, and had turned in to try to sleep,. So when Alice told him in a note that she had had enough, he understood. No hard feelings. Afterward, all he had to do was to give her a settlement that took all he had left.
"How did you find me?"
"I read in the papers about your appeal and about your success with it, and asked someone in your former chambers to find your phone number for me. I figured also that your address would be on papers you had filed, and, I was quite surprised to find you at Cav Neumont Manor with a proper butler and all. I take it that you received my message."
Through a long pause heavy with warning, Horace Hobby could hear her breathing while she hesitated to say that which he expected her to say next. And she did.

"How did you make that connection? Did you win that much that you've joined royalty?" She issued a laugh to indicate that she was only kidding, when in fact Mr. Hobby knew better.

"Indeed not, dear. I've been let a room at the manor, but I may soon be moving to a cottage on the estate." Light discussion with Alice was all right, but he wanted to get to the reason for her call; otherwise, other than learning that she was well, he wanted to get off the phone.

"You've been living in a room! How droll."

"Quite, but most comfortable."

"And will you be starting your practice again?"

"Yes."

"And can you manage it from a cottage?"

"I haven't thought that far ahead, Alice. It takes time to contact solicitors, meet with them, learn whether they will work with me . . . and so on. I haven't thought about where to live; other than realizing that I *could* actually work from the cottage. During the month that I've been here, I've come to enjoy the countryside and gardens, As well, I find I don't miss London noise and traffic."

Their conversation went on in this manner until Alice said she would love to have lunch with him, see him, hear about things, find out how he managed to turn around his case—she had thought the files were sealed—learn what he had been doing since. "I want to hear about the family who took you in," she said. "Or did they take you in? Perhaps they hired you for something. I want to hear all about it."

Mr. Hobby gave in. He would give her that time. "I was asked to be security on the kitchen floor; in the rear of the building."

"Security! How quaint!"

"You might have read in the news . . . recall the pipe bomb . . . that the family had ghastly problems; they needed tight security. Then, when I was in need, I

157

accidentally bumped into them and was invited to stay at the manor." He had no need to go into his days keeping warm and dry while having tea at New Chance. Nor would he tell Alice about sleeping in his car. Nor could he think that she cared. Apparently, Alice Hobby had not closely followed the explosion at Parliament; she seemed not to be familiar with the facts.

"Horace, indeed you have landed on your feet as I always knew you would."

Knew I would—he said to himself—she had had no such thought.

"And, I want to have lunch with you and hear all the details," she said. "I would love to see your village; it sounds charming: Cav Neumont . . . I looked for it on a map. I'm in Gates-Opening, not *all* that far away. I'm free tomorrow; I'll drive over. Where can we meet?"

His answer slowly crawled out of his mind and mouth—having a meal with her was something he had no desire to do. He had been wounded and still felt that he had open scars; some she had slashed. "The Meridian Inn is always a good choice," he said. "One o'clock, shall we say? Thus you won't be late driving back to Gates-Opening." This was giving her warning that, should she think it, he wouldn't be asking her to stay over.

"One it shall be," Alice said. "I'm eager to hear all about everything. Goodbye, love." She hung up.

Mr. Hobby's head ached; he hated the *love* part. Inappropriate. So out of place. She had a lot of nerve. How could he have been married to a pretty woman for twenty years and not miss her? Not look forward to lunch with her? Alas, he couldn't remember whether the marriage had been happy. Probably not. He had been rather dazed when she packed a half-dozen vans and left. As well, he had, looking back, quickly recovered from her not being there. He had to admit—he had not missed her. He must go to the kitchen; perhaps seeing Heather would soothe his headache. He could imagine that as he sat watching her at work, she would give him a glance, and he would hold her gaze as long as she would allow. They would work in silence, apart, but together, he felt, and thought she did as well. Then he realized that he must tell her he would miss lunch the next day. Missing a meal with Heather was intolerable, he thought, at least for himself; he couldn't speak for how it would be for her. He loathed saying it, but he must.

"Mrs. Ogilvy . . . he referred to her in that manner in front of the other cooks . . . I loathe to tell you that I will not be here for lunch tomorrow. However, I won't be far away and you can count on me to be here for dinner." There he had said it. Now he looked at her to see her acknowledgement.

"Why certainly, Mr. Hobby, and you enjoy yourself, though it won't be the same for us." She gave him a smile of understanding.

He wouldn't mislead; he preferred to be open and honest. "If you must know, although I'm sure you have no desire to know, being the polite and reserved woman you are, I have reluctantly engaged myself to dine with the former Mrs. Hobby. Her idea, not mine. She called me here, and she's driving over from Gates-Opening. She wants to see the village and the manor. The woman left me when I was bankrupt. Still I think that having been married to her for twenty years, I'm required to show her about, as she has specifically asked." Was it possible, he wondered, that for an instant undetectable by all but the most perceptive, Mrs. Ogilvy's face grew dark. It didn't occur to him, as it was the last thought in his mind, that Mrs. Ogilvy might fear that he and his former wife were on the verge of renewing their vows.

"We're meeting at one, and I shall have dined her properly, shall have driven her around the manor's grounds, and . . . I feel I must warn you . . . should she insist, in and out to see where I've been living, and back to her car in the village by four; better yet three. Then she's on her own. If not . . . please poison my dinner."

"Fair enough," Heather Ogilvy said. She didn't like this at all. Horace with another women? Showed that she cared for him more than she wished. After all, he would likely be moving to London where she knew he had been important in the past and would be so again. Well, she had always thrived on cooking for the manor, and she would continue.

Mr. Hobby's lunch with Alice Hobby went fairly well; though as he asked her about her life, had she remarried? he assumed not—no ring—he found he had no enthusiasm for the facts. He was not interested, and had to work to appear so. She asked all about the village and he told her about the success of the thrift shop, New Chance, that Lady Haversham had started. He struggled to stay on general topics, to keep Alice thinking about ordinary stuff, for she had placed her hand on his, which made him nervous. She was still pretty, shiny soft hair curling around her face, and large eyes open wide enough for a man to dive into. And elegant. Overdressed for the village; a silk dress, he thought, and diamonds. Diamonds of course that he had bought for her years ago. But nothing about her reached out to touch him; he found nothing of his original attraction from twenty-plus years back. He listened to her little speeches, and answered her questions. And when she asked where had he been staying before he met the Havershams, he merely said—in the village. She didn't need to know that he had been nearly penniless. Besides, he knew that, in her heart, she hadn't cared. It was all too apparent that her interest throve only in good times.

"I want to see the manor and your room now," she said as Horace paid their tab.

Futilely he had hoped that she was eager to drive back to Gates-Opening and had changed her mind about seeing the manor. He had actually ordered desert to draw out the meal, hoping to make her over-tired and over-full.

"Yes. Of course," he said with a restrained yawn, unable to conceal his own tiredness. "It's just a ground-floor room down the back hall from the kitchen. An appropriate location for a rear guard to live. Quite cozy, though, fireplace and all, and I have a woodpile nearby for my use. I eat with the staff, and all of my meals are tempting. The kitchen staff are my friends."

"You dine with the staff! How fascinating." And she pulled a face that said dining with the staff must be the most wonderful experience in the world.

He had driven to The Meridian Inn in one of the manor's golf carts, and now with it he drove her to the manor. It was still sunny when they arrived, a slight sun, faint, but determined to hold on to the day; a good part of his plan, for he could take up some of the time by showing her the wonderful vegetable garden. However, once they were there, he found that he thought of it as Heather's garden and walking about in it with Alice was a sacrilege.

Heather Ogilvy would have agreed, had she been asked, for as she walked to the rear door to see who had arrived, she could see Horace and a woman heading toward the garden. *Their garden; where they walked; Horace and she.* And now he was with another woman, and an attractive one at that. How could he not be captivated? Once again Heather had to remember that it wasn't her business. He had never told her that his feelings were particularly for herself. He was a free man. An attractive bachelor and out of her league. She turned to the chopping board.

Soon Horace Hobby and Alice, came in to the kitchen; Alice still enthusing about the garden. He heard the effort she put into pleasing him, encouraging him to think of her as the sweetheart she had once been. He was not fooled, he knew she had no interest in vegetables in their growing state—unlikely to recognize them. And as they passed through to his hallway, he said nothing to the cooks. They appeared to be absorbed in their work anyway, and didn't look up. Perhaps Heather had said something to them such as—pay no attention.

His room was tidy, painted with warm colors and satiny-white trim, and papered with just the right pattern. He stoked the fire in an attempt to find a way to pass the time. Alice Hobby looked around at his appointments. He asked her please to have a seat. Instead, she removed the scarf that was arranged around her shoulders, dropped it over a chair back, turned to him and clasped him in her arms.

"Horace, seeing you has stirred memories of our good times together. I've missed them so. I thought we were all through, but you know . . . we aren't."

He didn't know anything of the sort, and he gently peeled off her arms.

Undaunted, she said: "I've missed you. I want us to live together again. After I moved out, it took only a few months to realize my mistake, and then I couldn't find you."

Better to stop this right now, he thought. "Alice, you are a fine and lovely woman." He pushed her from him keeping her at arm's length. "And you deserve the best." He wished he could qualify that—*not the very best, but maybe a lesser best*—for she had left him at the time because his prospects were in the dump, he had always known that. "But it won't be with me," he said. "For I will never again make a sufficient income, and will always be looking ahead to the next check." This, he hoped was a slight exaggeration. "You wouldn't be cared for in the manner you deserve." He picked up her scarf, draped it around her shoulders, and then turned to the door. "Come,

Alice, by the time we get back to the village you will have just enough time to make your drive home before it's completely dark."

"But I had hoped to meet the family, and to see the cottage where you might be moving."

Under threat of death, he would not introduce her to the Havershams. Though Alice had the necessary social skills, he simply did not want to mix her with his friends. However, he had had no firm reason to object, when she insisted, to showing her the grounds, the vegetable garden, and if he must, his room. "I'll take you passed Firefly Cottage, but we won't be going in, I haven't the key. We won't be meeting the Havershams . . . they are extremely private and wouldn't welcome an introduction." This was pure fabrication—Sir Simon, and Lady Emma were friendly and out-going, and would have welcomed Alice, as she might merit, as Mr. Hobby's former wife; although Emma, he thought, would have her suspicions about Alice's motivation.

As they came down the hall and entered the kitchen, Alice, in a proprietary manner, hooked her arm into Horace's and enthused, "You said that these are your friends, the people with whom you eat. I want to meet them and give them my thanks for caring for you so well." And she gestured around toward Mrs. Ogilvy and the other cooks.

"Ah, yes, that's true," Horace said. "Mrs. Ogilvy, this is the former (he emphasized the word) Mrs. Hobby. She has come to check on me and to congratulate me for my recent success." He wished that Heather would recognize the mild sarcasm behind his announcement.

As Mrs. Ogilvy looked up, she was thankful that she not only wore gloves, but they were flour-covered gloves—she would not have to offer Mrs.—the former—wife, her hand. That went for the other cooks as well, and they kept to their stirring and beating.

"What a charming place to work. Amusing, I'm sure." Alice said, looking around. "I've not had the opportunity to work in a kitchen. Cooking is a good skill to help one get through life." She fashioned her bright eyes and uplifted eyebrows into an affectation of delight, but Horace could tell that Mrs. Ogilvy heard the dig. "I always thought these manor kitchens to be in a cellar," Alice said. "Didn't they wish to keep the kitchen staff below ground?" She waited for Mrs. Ogilvy to reply.

Thinking it was not her duty to inform this woman, Heather took her time to answer. "When Lord Haversham added modern features to the manor, he installed our kitchen here, as you see, so that we would be more comfortable and have windows onto the world."

"Then I'll give him my compliments," Alice Hobby said, "when I meet him. Soon . . . I expect." She gave Mr. Hobby a telling look.

Mr. Hobby hadn't remembered Alice's outlandish and embarrassing nerve: to assume that she would meet his lordship; to assume that the earl would care about her compliments!

As he and the former Mrs. Hobby were leaving, Alice called out in a loud way, "Goodbye all. We're going over to see Firefly, now," and she held onto his arm as long as she could; as long as he would let her. Much to his regret, he could feel Mrs. Ogilvy watching their backs all the way out to the cart. He burned with mortification.

Heather Ogilvy determined to never again, in a personal way, think about Horace Hobby. He was taken. The former Mrs. Hobby, refined and elegant, someone with whom he had history, would surely be chosen over her more simple person, a cook. Had he not understood Alice Hobby's put-down, that woman would now make certain that he did. He would fall back into his old life, not because of her disdain for the kitchen cooks, but because she was the elegant woman he could show off on his arm in

Chambers, or during festivities. Mrs. Ogilvy chopped harder, kneaded dough longer, nearly forgetting what she was about (for days the rolls would be tough), meanwhile wishing with all her heart that she had never met Mr. Hobby. She had been quite happy and settled, and now she would feel unsettled for a long time, perhaps until the end of her days. The other cooks looked at each other; they understood the sad place in which Mrs. Ogilvy tended her heart.

After depositing Alice Hobby back at her car in the village, Mr. Hobby drew in a breath of thankfulness to have the ordeal over.

Alice touched his cheek. "Please, let's do this again. I enjoy your company, and I want to hear all about how you are reestablishing your career. And I *adore* this dear village. Let's meet here again for a meal, Horace. And do let me know when you have access to the cottage. I long to see inside."

"We'll see, Alice." He almost tried to push her into her car. "I have no idea when I have to be in London; no idea what my schedule is going to be. I'll be in touch. Keep well, dear." He blamed himself for those words; words he hadn't at all meant. He had no intention to keep in touch with her.

He wanted to see Heather, but when he reached the kitchen, Tina said she had gone to her room for the evening; dinner already taken care of.

And so she had—gone to bed with sadness and confusion of heart. Although Horace had never, not in the slightest declared himself to her, she had some sense that they were becoming entwined. Foolishness, she knew, to have such thoughts, and once more she attempted to close her heart and to try somehow to find sleep. She dreaded meeting him in the morning, not knowing how to behave, how to look at him.

She need not have concerned herself about it for in the morning he did not come to breakfast. That night, when he reached his room, a message had come in through the manor that one of the solicitors, with whom he wanted to set up a meeting about future cases, was interested, and had time to meet early in the morning. Thus, in the morning, before the sun began its morning stretch, Mr. Hobby rose and set off immediately for London. He was there for the next three days. Every legal pundit in London whom he had represented before Court, had learned of his successful appeal, and as his reputation had always been of the highest quality, several solicitors wanted meetings with him.

In the morning, when Mrs. Ogilvy learned that Mr. Hobby had left, her face grew longer. Assuming that Horace's former wife lived in London, she imagined that Mr. Hobby and Mrs. Hobby, so used to moving about together in society, were renewing their former attachment.

Could Mrs. Ogilvy only have known that Mr. Horace Hobby went to bed in London each night with her face in his mind. He must ring her, he thought.

The day after her visit to Cav Neumont, Alice Hobby rang Mr. Hobby to thank him for the dinner and tour.

"I'm in London for likely three days of meetings," he said.

"I still want to see the cottage. When you return to the village, let's have dinner again and do try to get the keys so you can give me a tour." She realized that he had no enthusiasm speaking to her, but twenty years of marriage ought to count for something. She could be the social backbone of his career—she used to be. She decided to take a drive down to Cav Neumont, walk up Main and browse the shops. It would be her future hangout, had she anything to do with it.

"I saw that Mrs. Hobby today in New Chance," Hadley said. He was in the kitchen to add logs to the fire. "I was taking a look around, before returning. Lady Haversham had asked me to drive her in, and I recognized the woman Mr. Hobby introduced to us. It looked like that Mrs. Hobby was buttonholing Lady Haversham. I thought her ladyship appeared to want to duck, but the woman nail her to the floor with enthusiasm about how nice it must be to live in our village. Milady seemed to beg off to look around for a customer to help."

Hearing this, a squeeze grabbed Mrs. Ogilvy's heart. Things seemed to be moving fast, she thought. "And what did Mrs. Hobby do then?" she asked.

"Well, you know I had to leave, and didn't hear much more, though I did hear her mention to her ladyship something about seeing Firefly Cottage. Wonder what she has to do with the cottage?"

Mrs. Ogilvy thought she knew; perish the idea: Mrs. Alice Hobby is thinking about living there with Mr. Hobby. Perhaps that was the reason he had been gone three days now—they were looking over Firefly, mentally arranging it. She felt drained as though it would take super effort to lift her arm. Her life here, for which she had always had enthusiasm, might be about to change; about to enter a long, forever period of suffering. Of seeing Mr. Hobby—if he were about he would find time to visit the gardens and the kitchen, sometimes bringing that woman with him—no longer having him eat with her; no longer having him to walk with; how could she endure that? She must harden off her heart.

The phone ringing seemed to place a crack through the still room.

"Hello, Heather." It was Mr. Hobby.

She didn't know what to say to him—the hardening process was beginning.

"I'm in London," he said, "for two days or so for meetings. I may have found a solicitor I can represent in Court." Now there was silence over the line. He wasn't sure how to continue and felt slightly embarrassed that perhaps he had caught her at a bad time. "You know how it goes, I think . . . solicitors represent the client, and a barrister such as I am, represents the solicitor before the Judge."

"Oh, that's nice, Mr. Hobby." Within the business of keeping her heart closed, she had only half heard. He had talked about all that before; she didn't have to absorb facts anymore.

Now he felt more constrained, why her formality? These days, except in the kitchen, she never called him Mr. Hobby. He wanted to smooth over the problem, whatever it was, but was unsure how to proceed. He stood there, holding the phone to his ear, stuck for something to say. Could it be that she wasn't open to his saying anything. And, anyway, he was in a rush to get to a meeting.

"Well, Heather, I just wanted to catch you up, say hello, see how you were doing. I must run now." He hung up with a disturbed feeling from being unable to say the remainder of the speech he had in mind. It had been on the edge of his tongue to tell her he missed her, but her silence had caused him to feel awkward. He hadn't managed to say it. He needed to see her face.

She hung up puzzled. Really—why had he called? He actually had nothing to say. Mentally, she could see the Mrs. Hobby standing by him as he spoke.

But at that moment, the Mrs. Alice Hobby in question was instead at New Chance, standing by Emma, on whom she was trying to urge her friendship. She exuded her most polished social ability; let Lady Haversham know exactly who she was. She emphasized again that she was Mr. Hobby's former wife, and that they had been having lunches together. (Exaggerating—but Lady Haversham would not know that.) And that when he had the key, he would be showing her Firefly Cottage.

"I can't wait to see it. I know I'll love it!" An outrageous hint that she would be living there with Mr. Hobby.

Aside from wanting to escape the woman's effusiveness, Emma had no concern in the matter. She hadn't been apprised of Mr. Hobby's plans; knew that he had been offered Firefly Cottage, but so far had no idea whether he wanted to lease it. Her understanding was that he was interviewing solicitors, and was in the process of deciding how he wanted to go forward. He had said nothing about the former Mrs. Hobby. However, since he spent most of his time eating downstairs, and had to be urged on occasion to come up and dine with the family, Emma hadn't heard the latest.

As Mrs. Hobby looked around New Chance—wanting a new chance (she had to laugh at her word choice) to chat further with Lady Haversham—she took a seat at the tea table and poured out a cup. She watched customers browsing and occasionally asking for help. She watched Lady Haversham and Lady Mardling engaged in various activities: sorting, folding, hanging. Mr. Hobby had told her that the shop was completely run by volunteers, and that several people had a hand in helping it go. He had told her about the many donations from all over the county, for which customers from all over the county came in to buy. He had told her about the windows that Lady Claire designed, and that her window designs were drawing attention. And while Alice Hobby sat and watched and remembered, a new idea sprang within her scheming bosom. She waved goodbye-fingers to Emma, who acknowledged the wave with a nod, and Alice Hobby left the shop so excited her mobile was up to her ear as she hit the pavement. She immediately left an urgent-sounding message on Horace Hobby's mobile.

And when he rang her back, she enthused, "I might become one of the New Chance volunteers," she said to her former husband. She didn't miss the gasp he let out. "Yes. I've been needing something important to contribute to," she continued, "and this will be it. I *adore* New Chance. It's so amusing!"

Closing in, he thought. Her declaration and fake enthusiasm wearied him. He wished he hadn't given her his mobile number. It seemed she thought she had rights to close and personal contact with him. Not at all what he wished.

"But Alice, you live in Gates-Opening. Won't that be quite a drive for you?" He said this to put her on notice that he didn't foresee her living in Firefly; *If* he leased it.

"Only for one day a week. That is . . . at first." She allowed an insinuation to waft over the line. "So, I visited New Chance today, looked about, had a chat with Lady Haversham . . . she's *so* divine . . . I'm sure we'll be best friends. She was quite busy though, and as I sat with a cup of tea, and watched her interact with customers, I just knew that that was what I should be doing."

This was not news Horace Hobby wanted to hear. Although he couldn't imagine Emma establishing Alice as one of the volunteers, she might not understand his position with Alice; might mistakenly think he would like for her to hire Alice. He'd better head off Emma. He simply had to find the proper occasion to do so.

"And did you mention it to her?"

"Not yet, dear."

To proceed with her fine idea, Alice Hobby visited New Chance again. This time she asked Lady Haversham to have lunch with her. Though Emma had already found the woman to be tiresome, her thought was that if Alice Hobby would be joining Mr. Hobby in his new life, perhaps she should not turn her down; at least not emphatically so.

When the time came for lunch, Emma looked back to the tea table where Alice was waiting, and beckoned her to come; she could leave for lunch.

After they had taken a booth at The Bucket Arms, and after they had scanned the menu, and after they had placed their order, Emma looked up at Alice as though to say, and exactly what is it for which you have pulled me away from my work?

Alice began. "Lady Haversham, you were so clever to start New Chance. I can see that it's become a star; a popular gathering place for the village. Since I've been there, I have thought of nothing else. I *must* be allowed to volunteer there one day a week. That is at first, unless right away you need someone for more than that, and later on I hope to ask for two days." Hope-filled, she looked at Emma expectantly as if Emma were about to say, Of course, dear. We'd love to have your help.

However, Emma had become a guardian of all things New Chance and Cav Neumont Manor, and in such position, she had learned caution. Mr. Hobby had not said anything about joining up again with Mrs. Hobby, but then they had not had a conversation lately—not for the past week or so. And there was something desperate about the woman facing her: perhaps not desperate, but certainly pushy. Would she work out at the shop?

"Quite sorry, but I'm afraid not." She tried to soften this rejection. "Not at this time . . . New Chance has all the staff it can manage. We would be tripping over each other."

"Right. Fair enough," said Alice Hobby after giving herself a few seconds to realize that her proposal had been turned down. "But I'll be around and when you have an opening, do please remember me. Better yet, I won't let you forget, for I enjoy the shop, and I'll step in often; bring in donations." Alice Hobby managed to keep the pleased look on her face that she had been so careful to start with: her smile, her large, bright eyes, but her thoughts were that her scheme to volunteer at New Chance might not be the shoe-in she had expected.

"I'm eager to tell Horace that you and I have had lunch together, and that I've offered to volunteer at New Chance. Indeed, he will be pleased." *Add a bit of pressure*.

"I do thank you for your kind offer, and I'll take your card for such time when we might have an opening," Emma said. Would Mr. Hobby be pleased, she wondered. It sounded quite as though he was in fact teaming up with Mrs. Hobby. Well, he would have to understand that they didn't have an opening for a volunteer, and—though she wouldn't say it to him—she thought she would not ever be inclined to ask for Mrs. Hobby's help at the shop. Just not their sort, somehow. Other than her exaggerated effusiveness, there was nothing about the woman that was inoffensive—just not their sort. Not something she could explain. Just not their sort.

Horace Hobby had been reluctant to ring Mrs. Ogilvy again. He keenly felt the strain coloring the last call, but he needed to see her and would set up no more meetings in London until he had a chance to be in Cav Neumont for a few days. Test the wind. He thought he had found the right solicitor to work with, someone he knew well, and he could take a few days at the manor to think about where he wanted to live: Firefly Cottage or London. He wasn't comfortable with the thought of living where he couldn't regularly spend time with Heather Ogilvy. Besides, as barrister, he could take cases when he felt like it. He should be financially comfortable, he reasoned, and would have no need to take one case on top of another. And, if he leased Firefly, he could still take cases in London. He wanted Heather to see the cottage.

He packed his bag, paid his bill, and headed back to Cav Neumont and the manor. He could hardly wait; the country, his room, the garden—and Heather. He had been so busy he hadn't had opportunity to realize how much he missed his time with her.

Leaving London early, he arrived at the manor just after lunch, and drove around to the rear, his usual parking space. Another car, looking slightly familiar, was parked there. Where had he seen that car before? Then it came to him that it was Alice's. What was she doing here? Just what he needed when he wanted to talk privately with Heather! Although he had expected that Heather would be busy starting dinner, he wanted to ask her to take a short walk with him. Just a short walk: that would set him up for a bit. But now, Alice? He went in, his heart feeling disappointment and dread.

Alice was sitting at the kitchen table talking to Heather. Talking *at* Heather would explain it better, for Heather tended to chopping something as best she could, while Alice jawed at her constantly. The jawing was about Firefly Cottage and living there. How she would love to live in such a place. Horace Hobby understood that Alice thought she was talking her way in through a round-about manner, whilst Heather was wishing she would go away.

"Hello all," he said, removing his jacket and hanging it on a hook nearby. "I'm surprised to see you here, Alice." He gave Heather's back a look of great longing that Heather Ogilvy couldn't see (but was clear to Alice). He wanted to embrace Heather, his best friend, he thought—but it wouldn't do. He realized that he should have left her a note, assured her that he would hurry back, and most importantly he should have embraced her before he left for London. But, he recalled, he had had no chance, for she had gone up to her room.

"My dear!" Alice said, and she stood to give him a hug, which he accepted, but only politely. "I didn't expect you so soon."

"Didn't expect me *at all*, Alice. How could I have known you would be here? Consequently, how could you have known I would be here?"

"Oh, I took a chance. I know you want to show me Firefly Cottage; (perhaps assuming that was true would make it true.) I've been telling Mrs. Ogilvy and her cooks how excited I am to see it. And Lady Haversham has let me have the key."

"Let you have the key!"

"Yes. And had you not come in, I would shortly have gone on over there without you."

Mr. Hobby could hardly contain himself. "Why are you so keen to see it?" He had to give Mrs. Ogilvy a silent message. "Are *you* thinking of leasing it? You could, you know. Of course, you would have to go through Mr. Britely, the estate manager, but, as far as I know, Firefly Cottage is available." He wished that Heather would turn and look at him so he could give her a knowing wink. The only recognition she had given him was a quick glance as he came in, accompanied by a 'Hello, Mr. Hobby." If she would look at him now, perhaps she would see how he had missed her.

"Dear, how you do go on, you know you sold me on it, and ever since, I could hardly wait to see it."

This was too much. Mrs. Ogilvy moved to the stove and began to stir a sauce that already had been finished, but another minute's attention shouldn't hurt.

Horace imagined that she wished they would leave the kitchen, leave her to the cooking, get out of her way. He walked over to where she stood.

She looked up to him briefly and said, "How have you been, Mr. Hobby? I hope everything went well for you in London." She continued to pay attention to the saucepan.

Alice Hobby quickly answered for him. "Oh, rest assured, Mrs. Ogilvy, it did. He's told me all about it. He'll be in the swing of things quite soon. His reputation has been completely restored. I'm quite proud of him. Solicitors are seeking him again for his Court performances. So famous."

The room's air began to hang uncertainly, not sure it had the right mixture, for during and after the former Mrs. Hobby's little speech, no one spoke. Mr. Hobby did a jarring, out-of-character thing for him to do considering the circumstances: he leaned enough into Heather to firmly touch her arm and linger there a long four seconds.

"Come, dear, I want to talk to you about plans I have," Alice said, beckoning him toward her. "Let's go to your room. I yearn to hear what's been happening for you in London. Our phone chat was too brief." She moved over to him and hooked his arm to pull him along. "I need a chance to tell you how Lady Haversham and I are becoming great friends."

He didn't move, but he turned toward her to ask, "You and Lady Haversham?"

"Right. It won't be long before I'll become a volunteer at New Chance. Emma and I had lunch together and thoroughly discussed it. She said there was no opening at this time, but I'm in line for the first opening that comes up." Looking bright and chipper, Alice Hobby said this as though for her entire life she had been waiting to work at New Chance.

Mr. Hobby had to find a way to keep Alice out of his life and completely, firmly so. He knew also, that this would take time. She was determined now that she saw his income returning. "Another time perhaps, Alice. At this moment I wish only to go to my room—alone—and rest. I need quiet downtime from the hectic activity of my past few days. Other than knowing I'll be working again, nothing else is decided. I must think things over. Do you have a wrap? I'll see you out. Where are you staying?"

She saw he was dead serious, and that she mustn't let her efforts lag. "Another time then, dear. I'm staying in the village at The Meridian. Call me later when you're refreshed." She had seen his leaning into Mrs. Ogilvy, but wasn't deterred. She knew something though, that others at the manor, especially in the kitchen, did not know: about Horace's sophistication. When she and he were married, they moved among the best; he would always need the right woman on his arm, not Heather Ogilvy of the kitchen.

After Mr. Hobby saw Alice out, he returned to the kitchen expecting to give Heather a genuine greeting—he desperately wanted to give her a hug. Not just a hug, but a tight squeeze and to say over and over, "I've missed you. I've missed you." But the timing for that had passed. And now this: his ex wife following him around, as though he had no control over anything in his personal life. He tried to think how Heather must feel; sensitive and intelligent, she must wonder how he could have lived with Alice for twenty years. Overbearing Alice butting her way into Lady Haversham's company, and into New Chance. My, how he hoped Alice wouldn't begin volunteering there. He had to find a way to speak to Lady Haversham. But how could it be done? He had had numerous requests to dine with her and Sir Simon, but how could he say *Kindly do not use my former wife as a volunteer*. He couldn't have known that, already, Emma had instincts against that action.

When he reached Mrs. Ogilvy, she wouldn't look up. She still felt the rush of warmth from when he had leaned into her. While he was seeing Alice out, Mrs. Ogilvy had stopped annoying the sauce that was already perfect, and had moved over to a chopping block to chop celery. He walked over and stood by her, but he made no other move—there had already been enough scenes for the cooks to witness. Mrs. Ogilvy couldn't look up; she concentrated on chopping as if she had to mince the celery out of existence. Fairly shaken, Mr. Hobby went to his room and sat down at his desk. He stared out the window and thought about the conundrum: he was becoming newly settled in his career, but newly unsettled in his heart.

23

Agent Collins told Simon that Edward Fitzpatrick is a Russian spy, and was originally put in Cav Neumont to learn whatever he could about Simon: whether he were alive or not." Emma spoke to Lady Southway with great kindness, knowing what disappointing news she had to hear. Emma had asked her to lunch at The Meridian in order to speak to her privately. Lady Southway, of course, knew about the men who had been captured at the manor, but had just recently learned that one of them was Edward. She thought this couldn't be true; there must be a mixup.

"I'm so sorry, dear Charlotte. It was clear that he showed preference for you, and led you on. Although, I *do* think he was truly devoted to you, nevertheless, his fabricated self helped him to work his way into our shop, into our friendship; he was not a science writer at all. Yet, I know, and indeed I observed, that his attraction to you was genuine. It must have come as a surprise to him, and he must be sad to lose your company."

When suddenly, and without notice, Edward had stopped coming to New Chance, Lady Charlotte Southway, expecting him any day, had begun to know that something was wrong: she didn't think it was like him not to have a word with her about what was going on with him. And today, this certainty, the knowledge that Emma tried to dispense with kindness, tore into that small place where Charlotte had tucked Edward, the place she thought might be to hold love. Off-guard moments in the past had caught her thinking he might be the one. The one to break the long spell of her recent years without the arm of a fine man to hold. However, although deeply shocked, she was used to surviving.

"I'll miss his company. But that missing will be strongly tempered by the awareness that he actually wished harm against you and Simon," she said. "A sad situation that in truth cannot be undone, no matter how I might wish it. Should I slip into thinking about him with fondness, that thought will instantly be overlaid with a thought about who he really is. And I'll quickly forget him."

As they left The Meridian, Emma gave Charlotte a tight hug of understanding. Emma saw that Charlotte would be all right; she had a generous supply of internal strength.

24

It was established that Mr. Hobby would indeed lease Firefly Cottage. Although his legal work in London had started off with a bang, he did not want to live in London. He admired the city, but had grown used to the quiet of the country, and had grown used to his closeness to Heather. As barrister, he could take cases as he wished. Now that he had won his appeal, his financial position was comfortable enough that he had no worry about a requirement to work constantly. He could manage trips into London, and have enough time off to relax at Firefly Cottage. He was relieved to have so much finally decided. What a jump from hopelessness! From looking toward a life of poverty to re-acquiring the work and comfort he had struggled many years to gain. Sometimes he had to stop in his tracks to assure himself this was his new reality. He sat at his table with a cup of coffee as he projected what he wanted to say to Heather. He was keen to tell her the latest and had risen early to catch her before she got into sauces and dough. Perhaps she would be down now, and after checking his appearance, he walked down the hall to the kitchen. Heather was putting on her apron.

"Heather, with my practice beginning again in London, I shall either have to live there, or live here, and . . . wanting my own place, and no longer needed here as watchman . . . I am leasing Firefly Cottage. You know, you've heard so much about the cottage from Alice." He rolled his eyes: he meant this to be a dig at Alice's pushiness, but Mrs. Ogilvy didn't appear to hear it that way. A more serious explanation was in order. "I won't be required to be in London every day, or even every week."

"Mrs. Hobby sounds enthused about the cottage——." Heather began.

"Mrs. Hobby has nothing to do with it," he interrupted. "She will not be moving to the cottage." Ah, his first genuine opportunity to put things straight. "Although she may have spoken about it as though her name were already on its post box. I am standing here before you specifically to ask whether you will walk over to see it with me when you can take a break."

He ignored the other cooks who, with great interest, were looking at him. Heather seemed so astonished and speechless that Mr. Hobby felt the need to say more.

"Of course, I have already been through it, but that was days back and I want to refresh my memory. You know . . . what furniture it may need and such. Please do come with me, I'd like your ideas."

Heather gathered her wits about her quickly and said, "Indeed, I have heard, almost continually about Firefly; there seems to have been no other topic lately around the manor. And, yes, I would like to see what all this fuss is about." She ignored the inquisitive gazes around her. Her staff had attempted to disregard this exchange between Mrs. Ogilvy and Mr. Hobby, but clearly interest played across their faces.

"I miss our walks, Mrs. Ogilvy." He called her that when in front of others, or when his voice reached out more seriously.

"And I as well, Mr. Hobby," she was brave to say. She didn't feel so threatened now about the former Mrs. Hobby's interference. "I expect you know," she said, "that

Mrs. Hobby has been around whilst you were in London. She went down to your room for a while. Of course, what she does is not my business."

"I know. She rings me and did say once that she was calling from my room. Perhaps I should start locking it. I really do not like her invasions. Her sensitivities are not up to scratch I fear. I know that she pokes around to learn what I'm about."

He grabbed Heather in his arms, swung her around and said, "What I'm about, Mrs. Ogilvy, is taking you to see Firefly Cottage!" Realizing that his spontaneous act was rather out of character, and perhaps a bit overblown for circumstances, he released her and said, "Come, let's go immediately." He turned to see some of the staff laughing at his antics, and said mockingly, "I *must* see the cottage this instance! And if I cannot have Mrs. Ogilvy's opinions . . . for I have none of my own . . . I shall be entirely defeated and from then on I'll curl up under a rock . . . outside in the cold . . . catch my death . . . and it will be her fault! And if she says she can't leave now, I shall weep. I don't think you would want to see that."

And before Heather Ogilvy could speak, or resist in any way, he untied her apron, pulled it over her head, hung it on a nearby hook, took her by the arm and swished her down the hall and out the door. Ah, he thought, he finally had his walk with Heather; so pleased that she smiled a lot. He had caused that, and his heart was full.

Arm in arm they started down the lane, but when they reached Firefly Cottage, the former Mrs. Hobby, was sitting on the doorstep. Mr. Hobby almost felt his old despair. But realizing quickly that the situation wasn't that bad, his spirit rallied with the reminder that, if he remained stalwart, he had influence over the outcome. He was prepared to confront Alice once again; she was out of line, out of place.

"Hello darling, I was just on the brink of ringing you," Alice Hobby said. "I knew you were back, for I saw your car pass through the village." She stood, ready to go into the cottage with him. "Hello, Mrs. Ogilvy," she said. "I'm sorry that Horace dragged you along. He and I have important issues to discuss."

Heather's face fell dark. "Never mind," she said, "I'll just head on back. I'm needed in the kitchen, as it is."

"Heather," Horace Hobby said. "You'll do no such thing. Now that I've managed to get you here, you will stay and see Firefly, and give me your thoughts on arranging it. Heather stays," he said with a firm look to Alice.

"All right, dear. Let's do have her opinion," said Alice; stalled but not defeated.

He wanted to summon the rudeness to tell Alice that he had not expected her to be here, did not want her to be here, and wasn't at all interested in her opinion. He wanted to summon the courage (and he would get to it once again) to say her life was to be found elsewhere, not with him. But courage for these thoughts failed him and with a sigh, he unlocked the cottage door, and stood back for the women to proceed him in.

As he stepped inside he said, "Of course, standing empty as it has for a while, it's chilly and damp—,"

"But we can shortly fix that with a good fire," Alice said, interrupting him. "I saw that large wood pile outside. Let's get one started."

"No, Alice. We do not have time to stay," he said, another sigh escaping. "And I'm not yet ready to move in."

"I see," she said, and with a take-possession manner, she looked around, moving from room to room.

Mr. Hobby stood in one spot, just inside the door as though waiting for her to leave so he could go about his business. Heather was afraid to make a move as though she were waiting for her orders. They could hear Alice from another room call out, "Just here, dear. Come look. I see the perfect spot for your hand-carved mirror."

Hand-carved mirror! He hardly remembered it. Alice could keep it. And not here!

Alice returned to the front room and stood thinking, hand to chin. "I have the perfect recliner for that corner, Horace." She looked at him with triumph.

"I'm sure you do, Alice." He tried to rouse himself out of his stupor. "Come, Heather let's see the bedrooms and kitchen. I think they've been modernized sufficiently." He took her hand and pulled her into another room, but his keenness had been left at the front door. Taking a quick look around, he said, "I've had enough for this day; I'll walk you back, Heather. Come, Alice, so I can lock up."

"Yes, dear. Though I want to come another day as well, to see how it's going to work out." She saw the glare he fixed on her, "for you, of course," she added. He was not to be rushed—she understood.

While he held the car door open for Alice, Heather walked on toward the manor—let him say goodbye in his own way without her observing. Defeated for now, Alice said goodbye, issuing her lovely smile for Horace, that smile that had drawn him in in former times. She drove away thinking she had just begun; he would mature out of this initial resistance, and find that he needed her in his life.

He watched her drive off. He didn't know whether the tight head he felt was from foreboding, or from the tension she caused. He worked to relax; relax his brain, his heart. He turned down the lane toward Heather and caught her up.

As they walked back to the manor, Heather felt the difference in him; felt his anger. He has issues to work out, she thought. She regretted that they had had no chance to examine the lovely cottage in the way it deserved; something in which she could not interfere.

He continued walking in silence, too angry to release his emotions. Then, finally, "Heather, I regret that we couldn't give Firefly a proper inspection. Please save another time for us to do that." He could say nothing else. Time would have to pass. Then a better thought occurred: "What if after dinner, we were to again sit before the kitchen fire for a nightcap? We can discuss what we've been doing since we last talked. Seems like last year. And tomorrow I shall have to be in London again." He missed her smile; he wanted to see the fire flickering on her hair with it let down, but with his ex-wife's interruption, up until this moment he had been too annoyed to think about such gentle things.

"Yes, let's do," Heather said.

And so evening finally arrived. After Mr. Hobby had tried to work, but had yearned for the long day to turn to evening, after Heather had struggled to focus on sauces and stews, after dinner had been served upstairs and down, after the dishes had been removed, after the kitchen had been cleaned until it shone, they sat before the fire, feet propped up, relaxing, taking warmth from eachother. She wore open shoes and he could see her pretty toes; she had taken the time to decorate their nails with red enamel. He was surprised to learn how easy it was for him to love every feature about her down to her toes.

"I'll move my things to Firefly during my next break," Horace announced. "I feel quite pleased with my decision to live in Cav Neumont and control my caseload more than I used to do. And I've learned that I prefer a simple lifestyle." He looked at Heather with an intent that seemed to say, *this message is meant for you.* "The profession of barrister can be demanding socially," he continued. "Many events to attend. Dull indeed, but at times they provide necessary connections; even among the wives, sad to say. It's all politics." He sipped a glass of Port

185

while he watched the flames dancing about. "I'll return the parties once a year, no more than that, and I've arranged my chambers to that end. Someday you and I will escape to the city and I'll give you a tour."

Could he be letting her down gently she feared; preparing her that, for the greater part, he would soon disappear from her life? Perhaps he was letting her know that he would need a sophisticated woman such as Alice to help him with the requisite entertaining in London. She waited to hear something about Alice: would she successfully work her way in to the cottage, and into chambers? He did not bring up the topic again.

"Did you have a chance to see the cottage's beautifully outfitted kitchen? I know how to cook . . . I want you to know, Heather . . . and I intend to cook up soufflés and all kinds of exotic dishes." He laughed. He wished he knew how to make her laugh as in weeks past. But she continued to look rather severe. He looked at her; she nodded approval.

"Heather, you're taking me too seriously. The last time I cooked, I think it was oatmeal. I'm quite skilled with oatmeal."

His mobile rang. "Please excuse me . . . I think with all the balls I have in the air, I must answer it, otherwise you know that I would not. In fact, normally I would have left my mobile in the room." Without looking at the phone's readout, expecting the call to be about business, he said, "Hello." Then, "Fair enough. I'm busy now. Let's talk about it tomorrow . . . I'll be in London, ring me early."

He hung up and said, "That was about furniture. Alice still wants to talk about furniture: a few pieces, originally mine, that would be lovely in Firefly Cottage." Each time he had to deal in any way with Alice Hobby, he was left feeling drained. Whereas before the call he wanted to say so much to Heather, now all that had been flattened. Would have to wait.

Sadly, Heather thought she understood.

Schrödinger had arrived for his nightly kibble treat, and with melancholy that went undetected except by Schrödinger, who knew it was not because of him, Heather rose and went to fetch his treat. While Horace watched, wanting to go over and hold her close, she dropped a small handful of kibbles into Schrödinger's dish, and petted the cat. "I must turn in now . . . it's been a long day," she said. "Good night, Mr. Hobby." And before he had time to detain her, she quickly left the room.

Horace Hobby was in London for the next two days. Once his new chambers were finished, he wouldn't need to stay over in the city, but so involved with tradespeople and solicitors as he was, staying over saved time he could put to use. During these days, the fact that Alice Hobby was energetically at work visiting New Chance, and enthusing to Emma about the lovely Firefly, was causing much commentary in the evening as the Havershams and the Britelys discussed the woman.

And later, as Hadley sat down with the staff for dinner he announced, "Upstairs, they're talking about the cottage being leased again. I thought Mr. Hobby was leasing Firefly, but it seems his former wife is contracting for it." He looked around the table for someone to say something, but they merely swapped glances. "Doesn't that mean she and he will be moving in together?" Hearing only bits and pieces of the drawing room conversation as he was adding a log to the fire, he had misunderstood.

"Isn't that news?" Hadley asked.

"Actually, no," Tina said. "None of us wants that woman around. She's on the coattails of Mr. Hobby. Won't leave him alone."

Hadley looked at Brooks for confirmation; Brooks nodded agreement.

"I see. Looks like things are about to change," Hadley said.

No one could look at Mrs. Ogilvy. They well knew how she felt about Mr. Hobby. And they had seen that he felt the same. He should make a move for Mrs. Ogilvy, they had whispered among themselves. Soon, when Mrs. Ogilvy left the kitchen for a moment, their whispers spilled out into words.

And when Mrs. Ogilvy returned to the kitchen, Brooks said, "The man has been through much unpleasantness the past year or two. He has lived through turmoil, has been broken, lost everything, his wife left him, and now, through the help of the Haversham's, he can see light through all his problems. He's probably too shell-shocked to completely know his heart. It's time for him to move slowly." Brooks hoped Mrs. Ogilvy clearly heard his little speech, took it in, and absorbed his caution. He had heard the kitchen staff talk among themselves, had heard the chatter that Mrs. Ogilvy and Mr. Hobby were forming a close attachment. It was hard to look in her eyes now—she couldn't camouflage her disappointment.

When Mr. Hobby returned from London, he found a note on his door. It read, "Mr. Hobby, please do us the honor of joining us for dinner," and it was signed, Emma. It was early enough; he had time to change and to be upstairs in time for sherry. He looked forward to conversation with Emma and Simon, and whoever else might be there. First he wanted to speak to Heather, but she hadn't been in the kitchen when he came in. When he was ready to go up to dinner, as he went through the kitchen, he asked Tina, "Where is Mrs. Ogilvy?"

"She's on holiday," Tina said, with a look that implied, *you mean you didn't know*? She thought Mr. Hobby appeared a bit perplexed.

"I see. And when will she return?"

"In a few days, I think. Gone to visit her sister."

"I see," he said again. He turned away to hide his disappointment and started down the hall to the stairs. He should have called Heather while he was away, he thought. He shouldn't have let the challenges he had in London, and the frequent calls from Alice trying to take over his life, absorb all his thinking time and energy, such that at night he dropped right off to sleep remembering those things left undone that must be done on the morrow. Today, however, his legal and chambers' issues were finalized, and with a light heart he had eagerly rushed back to Cav Neumont expecting to find Heather, hug her, swing her around in his arms, and tell her all the important things that had to do with him. And with her.

"Mr. Hobby, it's so good to see you," Emma said. "We don't have your good company often enough. Please tell us what you have been about."

Sherry had been poured, and greetings had been spread around the group. Schrödinger watched from near Lord Haversham's shoes, and Horace Hobby relaxed into the comfortable fireside Queen Ann chair. He found good cause to smile; he took pleasure in this group of people, especially dining with them, especially when he couldn't eat with Heather.

"It's good to be back in the village, Lady Haversham. Everything went well in London. All meetings were beneficial, and I've actually received a case from my new solicitor, which I'll begin looking over soon. Quite good to be working again . . . thanks to you and Sir Simon's most kind help."

"Don't think of it, my good man," Simon said. "We've done nothing exceptional. Your reputation is the cause of your good luck."

Conversation about general things ensued for a while until Brooks announced dinner, and they went through. After dishes were passed and eating began in earnest, John Britely said, "What a marvel Mrs. Ogilvy is, organizing and training her staff so well. Here we are having excellent cuisine even when she is not in the kitchen, but off on holiday."

"Yes," Mr. Hobby said. "I hoped to speak to her when I came in, but she was gone."

"Oh, Mr. Hobby," Emma said looking at him with her eyes rounded as though she were presenting sparkling news. "Alice Hobby comes into the shop frequently." She hadn't meant to change the subject so abruptly, but it seemed to have been her first chance to learn what was happening between Alice Hobby and Horace Hobby. "She continues to offer to volunteer a day for New Chance, but sorry to say, I always have to tell her that we have no need for someone at this time." Actually that wasn't always entirely true, but Emma wouldn't say that she thought the woman was not a good fit for the Cav Neumont ladies. Just instinct; not certain why.

Mr. Hobby was much too polite and refined to denigrate his former wife, and yet he despaired of keeping the woman removed from his life. Their marriage had ended years ago, he knew that she wanted to renew it only because of his success—but he had been thinking about another woman for quite some time. And, indeed, had he not been thinking about the other woman, he still would not re-connect with Alice. He needed a way to convey this to the Havershams. And the way presented itself immediately.

"Mrs. Hobby told me about furniture she has that will fit beautifully into Firefly Cottage," Emma said.

"She's completely out of line," Mr. Hobby said abruptly, *time to take a stand*. "She and I have no understanding, and she will not be moving there. She might have some furniture of mine, but that can be her only interest." Finally! He had said it quite firmly and that should be the end of any thoughts of Alice's moving with him.

Forks and knives stopped clicking. Lips pursed. Eyes and brows around the table rose with surprise; not only the surprise that the union would not be taking place, but with surprise that Mr. Hobby would speak so plainly.

"I see," Emma said. "Fair enough, Mr. Hobby. When I see her next, I'll know to carefully guard against any suggestion to the contrary."

Nothing more was said on this topic. Emma and Simon were experts at removing discussions from an awkward air and restoring them to a congenial air, and good humor flowed around the table as forks and knives resumed their dance.

When Mrs. Heather Ogilvy returned from her holiday, Horace Hobby was waiting for her. He had been waiting for three days, sometimes pacing the kitchen, almost in the cooks' way. This didn't amaze the cooks, they thought they knew what he was about, and tried to stay out of his way. He had tried without success to phone Heather.

"Don't you have a number for Mrs. Ogilvy?" he had asked one of the cooks.

"No sir, we don't. She calls us daily to make certain there are no problems. I don't think she has a mobile."

He was in this way pacing the kitchen when she drove up to the back entrance. He had given up hope of seeing her this day, for it was nearly six already. He went out instantly and opened the car door.

"Ah, Mrs. Ogilvy. You are just the person I want to see," and he gave her a wide smile.

"Hello, Mr. Hobby, and how is that?"

"First. Let me say that you did not have my permission to leave. Especially without my approval."

She just laughed at him. She sat in the car with the door open.

"Next, I find it particularly maddening that you have no mobile, and I have searched the entire Earth looking for you."

"Why so?"

"I must move into my cottage and I need your advice and approval and blessings."

"Isn't Mrs. Hobby adequate to offer up those?"

"Shame! Why do you blaspheme my cottage so? My former wife has a court order not to stray within a two-hundred mile perimeter of my cottage. Our cottage. Oh, Mrs. Ogilvy how you have misunderstood, and I know it is entirely my fault." He had waited so long that he at last burst over with firmness and emotion; he was not to miss this opportunity. "And here you have disappeared from my life . . . my entire life (a little exaggeration wouldn't hurt) . . . leaving me in desperate need for a word with you."

Heather Ogilvy's eyes held questions.

He reached down for her arm, pulled her up out of the car and into his arms; he held tight. He was not about to release her.

Is this real? Heather asked herself. The warmth of his body was what she had thought about for longer than she wanted to remember. She had imagined how it would feel and now she had no need to imagine.

They were wordless until he said: "Mrs. Ogilvy, Heather, it has been you all this time who I hoped . . . nay dearly wished . . . would insist . . . in fact, would join me. Live with me as my wife in our cottage." There he had said it. He had to quickly push out his words; it did take some courage, but he had been working on that. He released her enough to look down at her. Then he removed his handkerchief to dab at a tear now working its way into her eye.

"Up until now, I just haven't been able to get the words out. And it's been agony with my being gone, and now your being gone. I returned from London ready to sweep you up . . . and you were not here! I've had to wait all this time to say this, to touch you, hold you, and tell you . . . ask you, will you join me?"

She held him for a few seconds—seconds that seemed an eternity to Horace Hobby, until she said, "Yes." And she held tighter. Had she not had so many ups-and-downs in her connection to Horace, she might have been more circumspect, but those very ups-and-downs assured that she would not hesitate. She knew her heart.

There was nothing else important to say now. He released her and reached into the car for her bag. With her bag in one hand, he took her arm in his other hand, and walked with her into the manor. His happiness swept over him like a loving breeze; he had had so many trials; he had been afraid she would not want to make her life with him. They stood a moment in the back hall while he held her again and dabbed her eyes with his handkerchief. In the flush of their emotion, it took courage for them to go into the kitchen to face the staff. He waited behind Heather while she said hello to the cooks, then quickly turning to the hall she said that she would take up her bag and be right back down.

He wasn't yet about to let her get away from him. He carried her suitcase up to her room where he gave her the long kiss he had waited for. Then he pulled back and asked, "Can you arrange to have dinner with me at The Meridian tonight? I have a great need to celebrate. Your excellent cooks can wait one more evening for your assistance. Please meet me downstairs in an hour." He was not going to accept a No.

"I would love to," Heather said, and she turned into her room. After she closed the door, she could only stand there. This was so sudden, and such an astounding outcome, she had to have a few minutes to calm down, think about what had just happened, gather her wits—his declaration had scattered them so. And here she had been thinking that he would never prefer her.

For a time, there were some who couldn't believe the wedding would take place. Particularly Lady Mardling, Lady Southway, and Lady Claire, who had had no way to know what had been going on behind their backs. Mr. Hobby, a man whom the Havershams entertained, a renowned London barrister, marrying the Havershams' cook? Kitchen Manager, some reminded them. Still . . . think of it! Except for the long-observant cooks, the news had surprised everyone at the manor. Simon and Emma had only a moment's surprise before realizing what a fine idea it was: two people with similar characters, whom they greatly esteemed, would now enhance each other's lives.

And as Emma was happily bring forth wedding plans, the marriage must be taken seriously. (Especially when people saw the diamond Mr. Hobby gave Heather.) There will be a festive tent off the front terrace, Emma said to anyone who was curious, and a simple but lovely chapel service. Cav Neumont, she mused, seemed to invite weddings.

"And was Heather Ogilvy to cook for her own wedding?" someone asked.

"Heavens no," Emma said. "Sara and Willa are coming in from Wickenbird Farm to help; they've already been asked, and are eager."

"Will Mrs. Ogilvy continue to cook for the manor?" the same someone asked.

"Heavens no," Emma said. "She will have Firefly Cottage and Mr. Hobby to cook for. Though she will supervise at the manor while the transition occurs. And perhaps help us out in a pinch, train our cooks when needed. Mrs. Ogilvy has already offered."

A word regarding the diamond: Both Heather Ogilvy and Horace Hobby knew no diamond had ever been thought of, or expected—it was just something Mr. Hobby had to do to express how his heart over-flowed with gladness. It took Heather Ogilvy, now Heather Hobby, weeks before she could wear the diamond, so unused she was to such glitter. Mr. Hobby understood. "Please wear it, dear, when we show ourselves at official functions. I want the world to see something of what I think of you: a small expression."

Though it was not clear at all whether she had been invited, Mrs. Alice Hobby attended the wedding. She was not yet done with Horace Hobby.

25

Tyler Brotherton settled into his flat in the manor's south courtyard. He had been hired to be a security engineer for the manor; to help them in any way he saw fit. He had discussed plans with Mr. Britely and with Brooks to install a computer-controlled gate somewhere along the road leading up to the manor. Since normally few vehicles drove to the manor—a few friends, family and service people—the gate shouldn't be an inconvenience. Of course it would only stop vehicles, not someone walking through the woods, but in time sensors would be added to the fields and terraces surrounding the manor. The Havershams loathed living in such a bubble, but the potential risk was substantial, and they understood that.

Tyler's flat wasn't all that far from the flat in which Corky and Troy lived, and that could be uncomfortable. Good thing that it was off a different courtyard, so he wouldn't often bump into Corky. However, he felt fairly blameless: he hadn't crossed any lines with her, had told her that he was a security engineer, which indeed he was, and it had been no secret that they met at The Bucket, and she had said that Troy understood. Perhaps, Tyler thought, he had flirted a bit more than was his want, but he had figured out quickly that he was in the wrong line of work, and had stopped meeting Corky. He had told her that he understood her position with a mate who studied late every evening, but he himself had warned her soon enough that he just didn't have time to meet any more. And, eventually, most evenings at least, he would be eating in his own kitchen. He didn't think she had been affected anyway and it wasn't too long before he saw that she had another man to buy drinks or dinner for her.

Sometimes he would walk the four miles to New Chance for a cup of tea, and there he would pet Major—at least when Major was there, for the dog would often decide to walk over to Firefly Cottage where his particular friends could be trusted to greet him warmly. Tyler would discuss the weather with Lady Haversham and sometimes with the Ladies Mardling and Southway.

The occasion for his starting to help, as a volunteer, was the day he dropped in when Lady Southway— Charlotte—working alone, was overwhelmed with customers. He stepped up to lend her a hand, took money and paid out change. The workload had grown accustomed to the assistance of Edward Fitzpatrick; however, sadly, he had met with ill fate and was not able to come in. Emma saw the need, and wanting to protect Charlotte from stress and overwork took it upon herself to ask Tyler whether he had any interest in volunteering to help Charlotte one day a week. Emma didn't say so, but she knew that Mr. Brotherton's salary from the manor would more than compensate him for his trouble. And a fact she didn't know was that lately Tyler was finding that he had a particular admiration for Lady Southway. He had often stepped in knowing she would be there, and he would furtively watch her while he had his tea. He thought she was lovely.

Although Charlotte was mostly adjusted to her loss of Edward, and hadn't cared to, nor expected to, find a gentleman to replace him, she was quite relaxed about having Tyler work with her. And in that unexpected, volatile manner in which the Universe evolves, it wasn't long before she noticed that Tyler had a special, intriguing fleck in his right eye when he looked at her. And sometimes, when they bumped together accidentally, she noticed that his warmth seemed quite special, was inviting. And it wasn't too long before he asked her if she would be so kind as to have lunch with him.

In time, Tyler Brotherton established himself in the Village of Cav Neumont as a security specialist. Security? the villagers asked among themselves. Security against what? But Mr. Brotherton ignored their questions, since for the time being he had all the work he needed conferring with Brooks about floodlights, cameras, and locks. It wasn't long, though, until the lady shop owners, seeing Tyler's square-cut jaw and cleft chin, realized the risk they had been taking by not installing the security he could provide, and he had appointments all over the county; that is when Lady Southway, Charlotte, would release him for the day.

In his cell, Edward Fitzpatrick went to sleep nights thinking, not about his failure to capture Lord Haversham, but about his loss of Lady Southway. Charlotte. As well, he had plenty of time to read the news and learn about the Hobby's wedding, which, aside from its association with Lady Southway, meant nothing to him. She would attend with all the other Haversham friends. Charlotte. He missed her. One makes choices and he had done his best, but perhaps that was a bridge he had crossed the wrong way.